D0744659

Middenrammers

✛

Midden-rammers

A NOVEL

John Bart

SQUAMISH PUBLIC LIBRARY
DISCARDED

© John Bart 2016

All rights reserved. No part of this publication may be reproduced, stored in a retrieval system, or transmitted in any form or by any means, graphic, electronic, or mechanical — including photocopying, recording, taping, or through the use of information storage and retrieval systems — without prior written permission of the publisher or, in the case of photocopying or other reprographic copying, a licence from the Canadian Copyright Licensing Agency (Access Copyright), One Yonge Street, Suite 800, Toronto, ON, Canada, M5E 1E5.

Freehand Books gratefully acknowledges the support of the Canada Council for the Arts for its publishing program. ¶ Freehand Books acknowledges the financial support for its publishing program provided by the Government of Canada through the Canada Book Fund.

 Canada Council   Conseil des Arts   Alberta
for the Arts   du Canada   Government

Freehand Books
515 – 815 1st Street SW   Calgary, Alberta   T2P 1N3
www.freehand-books.com

Book orders: LitDistCo
100 Armstrong Avenue   Georgetown, Ontario   L7G 5S4
Telephone: 1-800-591-6250   Fax: 1-800-591-6251
orders@litdistco.ca
www.litdistco.ca

Library and Archives Canada Cataloguing in Publication

Bart, John, 1944–, author
Midden-rammers : a novel / John Bart.

Issued in print and electronic formats.
ISBN 978-1-55481-318-6 (paperback).
ISBN 978-1-4604-0586-4 (html).
ISBN 978-1-77048-627-0 (pdf)

I. Title. II. Title: Middenrammers.

PS8603.A7717M53 2016   C813'.6   C2015-908604-3   C2015-908605-1

Edited by Don LePan
Book design by Natalie Olsen, Kisscut Design
Cover photo © Borzywoj | Dreamstime.com
Author photo by Suzanne Bart
Printed on FSC® recycled paper and bound in Canada by Friesens

To Sue

England
1970

1

THE COUNTRYSIDE WAS CHANGING, from soft-green trees to pale-yellow tawny scrub. An occasional thicket broke the northern flatness, a woody memento left by the South in its retreat.

It was not the rattle of the train that had awoken me, but a pervasive smell. The fat man sitting opposite me was pulling crescents off a large Spanish onion, which he then chopped into pieces on a tin plate that rested on his knees. He used an expensive knife with a whalebone handle.

I sat up and shook my head, the collar of my jacket grazing my neck. The train jumped and rattled again as we rushed through a station. Its platform was empty except for a porter, who wore a flat cap instead of the peaked ones worn by the porters at St. Pancras station. He pushed a barrow on which sat a solitary suitcase, and he was making much of it. I could tell he was badly paid. In the past I had behaved the same way and for the same reason.

My gaze returned to the fat man opposite me, and the small mound of onion on his plate. He wrapped the uncut remainder in greaseproof paper and stuffed it into the shopping bag that sat between his legs. From the pocket of his tweed jacket he pulled out a sandwich. The bread was thickly cut and the crust looked hard. The man bent his head, moving his hands over the food as if he were a conjuror performing a magic trick. He pulled apart slices of bread to reveal a clear cheese cut in roundels that glistened in the light, tainting the air with the clinging smell of unwashed feet. Immune to the rocking of the train, the man deftly slid slivers of onion onto the cheese, put the sandwich back together and took a large bite.

As he chewed he stared across at me with bold, bulging blue eyes. His ruddy features, edged with thinning grey hair, sported a white pencil moustache. He never dropped his gaze as he ate this reeking mixture in our small compartment. "You'll not be wanting to try it," he said, tapping the sandwich: a statement, not an invitation.

My head cleared. I rose, feeling stiff and awkward as I opened the compartment door and stepped into the corridor. "I'm for a beer," I said.

"Aye, I knew it. A southerner," the man said. "Booze before food. Suit yourself. Sweport in an hour. You think this smell is bad... Wait till we get there. Nobbut fish guts and sea spray."

I walked down the corridor. The onion man had the compartment to himself. Perhaps that had been his aim all along, I couldn't help feeling.

"*NOT MUCH TO SEE OUT THERE*," the barman said, "but bloody churches." He steadied a glass as the train lurched. The beer foamed. He nodded at the window. "I do this run once or twice a week. Winter and summer, looks as if the whole place has been scraped raw by the wind."

"You're not a Yorkshireman," I said.

"Not a chance... and neither are you."

"No."

"Staying long?"

"At least a year."

"In Sweport?"

"Yes."

"You'll get used to the smell, then. I can't. Where are you from?"

"London."

"This'll be a change, that's for sure. Rather you than me." He flipped the top off a second bottle.

"No thanks," I said.

"I'll join you, then," he said. "Barman's hazard."

The train reached Sweport. I collected my suitcase and climbed down onto the platform. People hurried past me.

I took a deep breath and choked — a thick, cloying smell made my eyes water and the gorge rise in my throat.

"S'bugger, isn't it?" someone said. It was the onion man. "You'll get used t'it happen, even though you're a southerner. Then again, mebbe not — it's fish guts, rotting on the dock." Passing me, he added, "Be quick, or you'll miss the cabs. Sunday buses are done. This isn't London." He trundled an expensive suitcase toward the exit.

I thought I heard him say, "Big girl's blouse," but I could not be sure.

As I walked out of the station a small elderly man got out of a weathered old car and called, "Dr. Davis?"

"Yes."

"Our new houseman. Come to liven up Sweport Maternity. I've been sent to collect you."

"How did you know I'd be on this train?"

He laughed. "My job to know."

"Who are you?"

"George. General dogsbody, telephonist, porter, know-all." He pulled a cigarette packet out of his pocket and offered it to me.

"No thanks."

I saw the onion man climbing into the back of an expensive car. In the driver's seat was a good-looking woman.

"Ship owner," said George, nodding at them.

"What?"

"Got money, knows what it can buy and knows the worth of everything to the last penny, like all of 'em. You look at that car. Got two steel I-beams running the length of the chassis. If you crash into it you'll crumple, but it'll be untouched."

I watched the ship owner leave. George lit a cigarette and coughed, his thin body contracting as if ratcheted on a spring. I liked him immediately. His wizened face, dark-lined from cigarette smoke, reminded me of the Parisian workers I'd gotten to know two years earlier. They had joined us at the end of the Sorbonne riots on the first march. Wry men with the lopsided smiles of experience, half mocking, half admiring the students who led them instead of following their elders and betters.

"The maternity hospital's on the other side of town," George said. "Hop in."

"It is?"

"Och, aye." He rolled down the window. The car started off with a jerk that made its body bounce on the springs.

"Shock absorbers," said George. "Next on the list."

"Och, aye?"

George grinned. "Gonna give as good as you'll get, eh? Thank God! The one you're replacing was too bleddy soft by half."

"What do you mean?"

"Couldn't take it. Wouldn't fight back. You'll need that where you're going."

"He'd be a big girl's blouse, then," I said in my best Yorkshire.

"Aye, 'appen he would," George shot back.

After a few minutes I said, "That's the second time we've passed this building."

George shook his head. "We're two streets over. Just looks the same. Same old houses, same style. Only difference is the supermarket on one street and the Post Office on another. You'll get used to it. S'all a one-way system in Sweport. To get across town you've to go back and forth like a shuttle in the warp."

We drove on. The streets were deserted except outside a pub, where people stood in groups. I heard laughter.

George said, "The road from Leeds to Sweport was built by the Romans. It's good and wide, but the port itself was cobbled together after the Black Death. They put the buildings as close as they could, God knows why, so the road's not wide enough for two cars. Just horses two abreast." He threw his cigarette stub out of the window.

I took out my packet and offered him one.

He grunted, lit it and took a long drag. "Mind you, it didn't have to be this way. The Germans bombed the devil out of Sweport during the war, flattened the docks and most of the town centre. Nothing but rubble left. After the war, the council — stupid buggers — rebuilt exactly the way it was before the war. Couldn't let Jerry dictate, could they?"

The car bounced over a pothole in the road, metal groaning. We stopped at a red light.

"Anyway, they like medieval round here. Fits their bill."

I said nothing. Cigarette smoke drifted out of the window. The cracks in the car's leather seat made it more comfortable.

"Cut our nose to spite our face," George added. "But that's us all over."

"You've a Scot's accent. How long have you been in Sweport?" I asked.

"Down from Glasgow twenty-five years ago, for the summer. Still here."

A seagull cried. I saw three of them swooping against the grey sky. I could smell the sea. It was cold when the wind blew. We started off again.

2

THE DARK BRICK BUILDING formed three sides of a square. The fourth, a low wall with iron railings set in the brickwork, had two tall gates that looked as if they were never closed; long tufts of grass grew through their bars. I caught the tang of the sea in the moist air and, occasionally, the horrid fish-gut smell that had threatened to choke the life out of me at the train station.

In the centre of the square several cars were parked in a cobbled courtyard.

"Visiting hours," said George. "They'll be gone soon."

In one corner of the quadrangle stood an off-white Daimler ambulance of World War II vintage, the ribbed chrome of its radiator reflecting the day in warped mirror images.

George walked over and put his foot on the running board. "I love this one," he said. "Out of place here, like me. We should be in Edinburgh or London, capitalizing. Instead we're in Sweport." He opened the driver's door and sat down.

"Does the hospital need its own ambulance?"

"For the Flying Squad. When there's a problem with a home delivery out we go, hotfoot to sort it, bells ringing," he grinned.

I looked at the hospital. Through the main doors I saw a nurse hurrying. On a balcony, jutting from the first floor, a woman in a hospital gown smoked a cigarette, an IV feeding into the crook of her elbow. Sweport Maternity had the same air of dilapidated efficiency of other hospitals where I had worked. Snapping Sisters in starched blue and white, their fiefdoms at the ends of long corridors with chip-marble floors that curved up gloss painted walls, all the corners rounded.

"Looks good, doesn't it?" said George.

"Och, aye."

"That way, Doctor." He leaned back against the driver's seat and pointed to a path which ran under the balcony, where the woman smoked.

Suitcase in hand, I walked past a sign that read, "Doctors' quarters. Private. Keep Out."

Around the side of the building were a set of post-war pre-fab houses, small concrete buildings with rain stains at their corners. Past them an open paddock, on the far side of which were the back gardens of small brick houses set in neat rows. Above everything a huge sky, the seagulls endlessly swooping and crying.

An Indian woman dressed in a red-and-yellow patterned sari passed me, a long, thick, black pigtail rolling sinuously from side to side across her back with each step. She was older than me by a few years. She turned and asked, "Are you the new SHO?"

"Yes."

"Oh, well, then. Hello! Jolly good to meet you." She held out a hand. "My name is Sunita. What's yours?"

"Brian Davis."

"Come on, Brian. I'll show you to your quarters."

We marched down the path together. It ended at the prefabs, which were uniform in construction, but with window boxes of different styles and colours.

"That is our house," she said, pointing to one with blue window boxes. "Yours is the one dressed in yellow. Tripti will be glad to see you. He's been working your shift to cover your absence."

"Tripti?"

"My husband," she said. "Dr. Chak. He is your Senior Registrar. I'm glad to see you, too, because now he'll have more time at home with the children."

Two of the prefabs had bare windows overlooking a couple of wooden picnic tables and a charcoal barbecue.

She said, "It's not your fault there was a gap between you and your predecessor. The administration could have organized things better, but they will do anything to save money. There is nothing new under the sun."

I heard a ship's whistle. A seagull landed on a picnic table, feet scrabbling against the wood. Sunita waved it away, the gold on her fingers flashing in the light as its wings beat the air.

"Tripti did not have to work all the hours that he has done today, but Sheila, another SHO like yourself, has a concert for which to prepare, and Arjun — the third one — couldn't work day and night for three days in a row, could he?" Sunita smiled at me and continued, "Tripti is a stickler for the rules. No thin cover on his watch. As it happens, the concert is tonight, so Sheila will be fully up to the mark by tomorrow."

She reached up and along the back-door lintel of my cottage. The fold of her sari fell back as she pulled two keys down, revealing her shoulder. The Hindu red spot in the centre of her forehead had small gold bars at its edges, tiny wings I had never seen before.

"One for you and a spare," she said as she passed me the keys.

Brown skin disappeared as she lowered her arm. "The scuttlebutt says you are not married, so you may not need it."

"No. I am not. What else does it say?"

"Come for supper, and we'll tell you. In one hour. Tripti will be back. Arjun is coming, too. It's a Sunday ritual we fulfill whenever we can. It'll be out here, on the picnic tables."

"Thank you, but..."

"I absolutely insist. Please do not refuse. It will be potluck, as usual."

She went into her house.

I opened the front door of my prefab and went inside. Everything was on a small scale. An entrance hall, a room to the left with a couple of elderly armchairs facing a gas fire, and, at the back, two bedrooms separated by a bathroom. To my right, the kitchen: a Formica-topped table, a stove, a fridge, and two kitchen chairs, all garnished with a strong smell of curry. There was a telephone table, but no telephone — I found it on the bare mattress of a bed in one of the bedrooms, the spear-shaped phone jack lying on the wooden floor, not plugged in. A set of sheets and two striped pillows leaned against the wall. There was no headboard.

Through the bedroom window I saw two people making their way along the path. One was a tall, thin Indian man with an elegant air and military mustache. The other, smaller man, also Indian, could have passed for a boy of twelve, except that he, too, had a thin, black moustache.

He swung an arm in the air and shouted, "Howzaat! Leg before! Over!" several times. "What a great bowler I am!"

I took a book out of my suitcase, lay down on the bed, and tried to read. I heard the two men talking for some time; then doors closed, and there was silence.

WE ATE OUTSIDE, as Sunita had promised. Tripti, the tall Indian, sat his baby son on his knee while his daughter fed her young brother his food. From time to time Tripti's gold watch, with its loose gold bracelet, slipped down his wrist, and the young girl would scold him and order him to keep it out of the baby's mouth.

The other, Arjun, the smallest and thinnest man I had ever seen, pronounced, "I am of the Brahmin class. That is why I am so elegant."

"You know everything. You have an opinion about everything, which fits so well with your good opinion of yourself," said Tripti.

"Of course. I am Brahmin!"

Sunita said, "Oh Lord! And he is smiling. This is why we did not go to India. Imagine having to put up with the caste system in all its glory."

I said, "*Go* to India?"

She said, "Tripti and I are from Uganda. As I am sure you know, things there are far from ideal for anyone who is Indian. So we packed up and came to England. We did not want to go to India. Too foreign."

"Must have been hard for you," I said.

"Oh no!" she said. "The rule of law applies here, the English law that used to run Uganda in the good old days. Which is exactly what we wanted."

"A general habit of obedience to the law is what counts. It is all that matters," said Tripti. "And the best is English common law. It is fair."

"That is also the way in India," said Arjun.

"Pull the other leg, it has bells on," said Tripti.

"My elegant friend, it is only a case of different rules, ones you don't understand. You would adjust in a very short time, trust me."

Sunita said, "Well, whatever, we are now in Sweport. England ... rules... they keep us safe. Without them there would be difficulties."

"Especially here," said Tripti. He gave the baby to his daughter and stood up.

"What do you mean?" I asked.

"They keep the peace. We have had problems with..."

Arjun broke in, his voice rising as he said, "Not just problems, Tripti, old son."

He turned to me and said, "We have had the Wars of the Roses and the Hatfield and McCoy feud rolled into one. Right here in delectable Sweport."

"You exaggerate, as usual," said Tripti.

Sunita held out her hand. "Tripti, you had best explain what Arjun is talking about. He is too excitable to make sense."

"Oh no! Let me!" said Arjun. "I am the best at explaining such things to an outsider."

I opened a bottle of beer. The wood of the picnic table was warm from the sun. Someone had carved a name in it over a heart.

"It is like this..." said Arjun. "Some years ago when we..."

"No!" said Tripti, "No archaeology, no old history. Leave it! No explanations."

The baby cried.

"Oh boy!" said Arjun. "The value of archaeology is to shine a light on the present."

"No! No!"

Tripti's daughter picked up the baby and went into the prefab. She had a closed look on her face. She walked stiffly, high stepping like a stork at the water's edge because of the bundle she carried in front of her.

Sunita said, "Look what you've done, you two. You've upset Rukhmin."

Tripti shook his head. "All right, all right, leave her to me."

"I can't trust you not to be clumsy, Tripti. I'll come with you." She stood, saying, "Excuse us, Brian."

"I should be getting to bed myself, in any case," I said, standing up. "It'll be an early start in the morning. Thank you both; that was lovely."

I AWOKE LATE in the night to hear a baby crying and the sound of someone's feet on the path. A pager went off, the beeps fading away as its owner walked to the hospital. A car engine came to life. A dim glow rose from lights around the cobbled quadrangle. Behind me, where the open paddock lay, was only darkness.

In the morning I found I had fallen asleep without plugging in the phone. I was in a strange place again, routine not yet established.

I WALKED INTO SWEPORT MATERNITY and climbed the stairs to the landing outside the Delivery Suite. Two women were talking as they took off stained green cotton coveralls: midwives leaving work. The coveralls opened at the back to protect the women's pale blue and white striped blouses from all but the worst stains.

One woman was undoing her companion's ties, then she turned to have her own ties undone. She wore surgical trousers; her companion, a short, loose skirt with pockets. Both had paper covers over their shoes. They stuffed the shoe covers into a bin and the coveralls into a laundry basket outside swing doors marked "Delivery Suite."

"Full moon tonight," said the first woman.

"You know what Woodie says: 'That's when they all shell out, like peas from a pod!'"

"Our leader loves it when we're busy. She probably puts Pit in Sweport's drinking water." Pitocin, a drug that causes the uterus to contract, beloved of all obstetricians wanting a weekend off.

As a student I'd often heard that the full moon caused women to go into labour. I had no idea if it was true, but it was a universal dictum. Medicine is full of sayings like "The full moon brings them out." David, a radical friend of mine, who, for a time when I was younger, had led me to a life of protest in Berlin and Paris, maintained that these sayings were ways of defining our ignorance. I wasn't so sure.

The women gave me a quick glance, then walked down the stairs that circled the old cage elevator. They had learned to ignore all but the task in hand — in this case, gossip. I heard one of them say, "Handsome is as handsome does," an expression that has no real meaning, but says everything. I wondered if it was me they were talking about.

Behind me were another set of swing doors marked "Keep out. Hospital Personnel Only." A tall, thin woman in surgical gear came through them.

"Hello," she said. "You're Brian Davis, aren't you?"

"Yes."

"I'm Sheila Tolwich, the other SHO. We've not met yet. Come through and get changed. I've been up all night — now it's your turn on the treadmill."

Through the doors were two changing rooms, a couple of armchairs, and a desk on which stood a kettle and a phone. On a shelf above were the makings for coffee and tea.

"Homely, isn't it?" Sheila said. "The fridge went on the fritz last week, so it's not much fun if you're thirsty." She sat down. "I'll wait till you get changed and take you through to the other side. Woodie's in full flight right now. All four rooms are busy. She's got a Pit drip going in two of them... Well, I should say, *we* got them going but really, she runs things up here, thank God, and we follow her lead."

"Woodie?" I asked.

"That's Sister Helena Woods, Senior Midwife," she explained.

When I came out dressed in scrubs Sheila was sitting with her eyes closed and her right forearm held upright. Her left hand was running up and down it, the fingers looking like a large pink spider mangling its prey. She opened her eyes and said, "I'm practicing the fingering for a piece I'm to play in a couple of weeks."

"What instrument?" I asked.

"Violin, of course. Didn't Arjun tell you?"

"No."

"Well, that's a first. There are no secrets around him."

"Why did you say, 'Thank God'?"

"When did I say that?"

"About Woodie. 'Up here she runs things, thank God.'"

"Oh... Because when she's left alone to run things she's great. She could deliver an elephant out of a fly."

"Alone?"

"She's a midwife, right? They don't need doctors to deliver babies."

"That's what they told me all the way through med school."

"And that's what all the midwives say, till they need the nurses and doctors. Mind you, Woodie's been running things on her own because Mr. Cooper's been away for a week. We SHO's have had bugger all to do up here. She sees to that."

"Cooper's one of the gynes, isn't he? I can't remember the name of the other."

"It's Leander, but don't bother to remember it. He's out of commission, and Tripti's doing his hospital work."

"How did that happen?"

"He had a stroke. Not surprising, really. He's an old boy."

Sheila stood up. She was a lot taller than I. She opened a small pebble-glass window over the table, and we could hear someone's voice below, but not what was said. A ship's horn sounded loud and clear, and a breath of cold moist air blew in. There was a patina of something white on the outside of the wooden window frame. I reached up and put a finger on it. Salt, left there when sea spray dried in the sun.

"One thing about Leander, though — he dressed with style. I once saw him in spats and pinstriped trousers, with a spotted bow tie and a winged collar. I don't think he's coming back. Time will tell. In the meantime Tripti's it half the time. But the other half... that's Mr. Cooper... He's running things. Finally. What he's always wanted."

"He's the one who signed my contract. There was another signature, too, from someone in admin."

"Burke's, I shouldn't wonder. Those two are getting closer by the hour."

We went into one of the delivery rooms. There were no windows. Pale-green tiled walls were lit by the large, mirrored, circular light that hung over the delivery bed at the end of the room. Steel equipment filled the space between the bed and the nearby incubator.

Directly ahead I saw a woman's legs in stirrups. Her exposed thighs gaped wide. Another woman, blond and trim-waisted, sat between them. She glanced round and then turned back, totally committed to the task at hand.

A midwife came in and said, "I'm free now, Woodie."

"Good. Let's get her legs down to make her more comfortable. You and Dr. Davis take one side each."

Sheila slipped out. I wondered how Woodie knew who I was. I helped the woman lower her legs.

"Put her foot on your chest, please," said Woodie. "And you, Mum, push when you want, as hard as you can. We're nearly there."

The woman pushed against my chest wall and grunted as her stomach bulged upward with each uterine contraction. The sweat running down her forehead matched mine as I braced against the leg that threatened to push me over with every wave of effort. Woodie said, "Push, push," and then quietly, "Now relax for a bit, love," over and over in a well-tried, rhythmical song of encouragement. Her forehead was lowered, level with the patient's gaping anus. Its pink rim, flattened against the oncoming head, became finer and finer with each exhortation. The baby's skull, which had contracted and expanded as it traversed the vaginal canal, was still firm enough to do the job of leading the way.

Eventually a small, black, wet curl poked out. The smell of meconium grew stronger, presaging the appearance of the baby's head. A few moments later, heralded by the woman's loudest scream, came the longed-for crowning.

The child's features were red and suffused, and its eyes were swollen shut. Woodie slipped a gloved finger behind the skull to make sure the cord was not wound round the neck. She gripped the head, twisting it clockwise as she pulled downward. A shoulder squeezed into view. Woodie slipped the same finger into the armpit and winkled out the arm. Then she twisted the baby's body the other way, so that the other shoulder came through and, immediately afterward, in a rush, so did the rest of the child.

The blue-and-pink, thumb-thick umbilical cord flapped against the delivery sheet, now covered in blood and a sticky grey fluid. Woodie grasped the baby's slippery heels tightly between the first two fingers and thumb of one hand. Supporting its body she leaned through the woman's legs to lay the newborn on its mother's belly.

She took a breath, then reached for two stainless-steel clamps and applied them to the cord, an inch apart and a hand's breadth from the baby's tummy, signalling for me to cut the cord between the clamps. It had a gritty, rubbery feel and was tough enough to impede the scissors' blades. I managed to sever it at the second attempt.

"Take my place," Woodie said, getting up off the stool.

I sat in her stead and waited with my fingers hooked over the remaining clamp. As I had been taught to do, I exerted a slight pressure until a rush of blood signalled that the afterbirth had peeled off the uterine wall. I could now pull downward to deliver it.

I felt something give, and the placenta squeezed out to flop into my lap, body-warm, heavy, moist, and meaty. Its surface was covered by a clear, bluish, toughly applied transparent tissue that curled round the outside of the cord.

I turned it over to see if any of the dark-red cotyledons had blackened areas. These would show where they had not been clearly adherent to the uterine wall, indicating a deprivation of blood and oxygen. This would have some bearing on the safety of the next pregnancy, if there were one.

Beside me the baby was being coddled and wrapped tight in midwife fashion and given back to the mother, who cried and laughed by turns, relieved, delighted — and ready to go through it all again if this were always to be the outcome.

IN THE HALF-LIGHT of the early morning, with the rush over, we sat together drinking tea and eating chocolate biscuits: me, Woodie and two other midwives. I could not take my eyes off her when she stood up, tall and fair, arms akimbo going over the deliveries.

"You weren't sure Room Three was face-to-pubes, were you, Joanie? I was, so I said we shouldn't let her push too soon, which is what they always want to do when it's that way round. Even so, till the head crowned you weren't sure, were you? She was one of the nuisance ten percenters who come out like that. Sent to try us."

The midwife, who looked like a farmer's wife, nodded.

"Were you really sure?" said the other midwife. "Why didn't you say so?"

"I was trying not to embarrass Our Joanie."

The three women laughed.

"You're never wrong, are you?" said Joan.

"No. I'm perfect. Look at me."

The other midwife, who sat closest by me, muttered, "Your face, my arse."

Woodie said sharply, "My arse, your face, more like, Irene. And you don't have to whisper. You have a comment, say it loud and clear. I can stand it."

I was struck by the sight of a shock of blond hair which had burst loose from under Woodie's cap. She moved easily, as if bone and muscle and flesh were always in tune with one another. She was older than I, but that didn't matter to what I felt. I was pleased when she said, "There's just one lass left out there. Dr. Davis, would you come with me, please, and we'll see how far on she is. She was three fingers a while back."

"Call me Brian."

"Yes. Thank you. But not in front of the patients."

"What shall I call you?"

"Woodie, like the rest of the world."

"But not in front of the patients."

"Right."

We left the others and crossed the divide between work and play on the way to the delivery room, where there was a woman well on in labour.

"That Irene never says things out loud. Always chippying on in the background. No guts," said Woodie. "I hate that, but what else do I expect? She's a cow-and-a-half, always has been. One of Corrigan's lot."

"Who's Corrigan?"

"You'll meet her soon enough." Looking angry, she added, "Let's get on with it, please."

The patient was six fingers dilated. She was small, dark, cheerful, and co-operative, which promised an easy delivery. Woodie and I stayed with her.

After a bit I said, "Mrs. Cawl, I think you're fully dilated."

Woodie put on a glove and, after putting her hand in the vagina, said, "There's a small rim of cervix at the top, Dr. Davis, trapped between the head and the pubic bone."

Our Joanie came in and said, "Just so's you know, Sister Woods... Tripti and Arjun have two more cases in the O.R. and one of them's a Caesar, starting right now. They'll be busy for a while."

"No problem," said Woodie. "Thanks for telling us. Keep an eye on things for me out there, will you? Me and Mrs. Cawl go back a long way together. I want to be here."

"Yes, love." Our Joanie smiled and bustled through the green swing doors, letting in the outside world for a moment.

Mrs. Cawl said, "I want to push. I want to push!"

"Good," said Woodie.

After fifteen minutes of straining and groaning hard against herself, and relaxing between efforts, Mrs. Cawl lay back to catch her breath. Woodie wiped her patient's forehead with a damp cloth.

"Roger still working?" she asked.

"Yes," said Mrs. Cawl. "Thank God."

"He'll not be doing the Christmas run, will he?"

"No. He learnt his lesson after what happened to your Joe. He's kept his mouth shut." She shook her head. "I'm sorry... I'm sorry to muck that in, but those middenrammers taught him a lesson."

"It's all right, love," said Woodie. There was a silence during which all I could hear was heavy breathing. Then she said, "It's okay, Clara Cawl. At least something good came of it."

"Sod them," said Clara in a flat voice and then, "Oh God! This one's worse! Oh Jesus! Oh God! Oh Jesus, I hope he'll come soon!"

But the baby did not; neither did Jesus. Thirty minutes later Clara was still pushing, and a little later it was clear that she was done. Between contractions she lay very quiet, sweat dripping off her. I put the trumpet-shaped stethoscope to her belly. The baby's heart was beating at a fast clip, about 120 beats per minute. He, at least, was not distressed.

Woodie said, "He's right there. Just a little more to push him through."

Clara was very quiet. "I can't... I need... I'm bleddy tired. It's been forever. You have to help me."

"It's forceps for you, then. It'll be a simple lift out with the Wrigley's." Woodie looked over at me and said, "Dr. Davis will do it. I'll tell you just what he's about, so you know what's going on."

Outside the delivery room I stood at the six-foot-wide, two-foot-deep stainless-steel sink. A row of taps with long handles ran along the tiled wall above the sink. There were cracks in the tiles radiating from where the chrome-bright but already-worn taps were set. Woodie slipped out and stood beside me.

"You okay?" she said.

"I've never done a forceps delivery," I said. "I've seen them applied, but never done it myself."

"Students generally don't," she said. There was a half-smile on her face. "Well, you're a doc now and the only one here." She leaned forward. "I'll guide you through it," she said. "I've done it before for beginners like you. Trust me."

She was so close, so definite, so sure of herself. I elbowed the taps open, first the hot, then the cold, ran the water over my forearms and pumped the soapy disinfectant dispenser. I lathered up to my elbows and rinsed off several times. Brown and yellow bubbles crowded the drain. My heart was in my mouth. I had not been this way since I went to the Royal College to get the results of my finals. Overwhelming excitement was the reason I had chosen a career in obstetrics. For me, from the first, delivering babies had been a long, exhilarating high. I wanted a life full of it.

Woodie seemed to know that. And as I stopped to catch my breath, hands wringing wet, I felt as if I knew something of her, as well.

I backed through the swing doors to the Delivery Suite. Wearing gloves, Woodie gave me a towel to dry my hands. Then she held open the green gown I was to wear, and I slotted my hands through the armholes. I turned for her to do up the ties, one at my neck and one lower down. Taking care that our fingers did not touch I handed her the long waist ties that hung down at the front. She tied them for me at the back.

As she pulled my mask up over my nose she said, "Glad you don't wear glasses. I'd have to waste a lot of time wiping the mist off them."

"We aim to please," I said.

I put on the latex gloves that lay open in their packet, peeling them off the paper backing to do so. I had to snap the fingers to get them to settle correctly. Finally, with the whole ballet routine over, I was what I was meant to be: incognito, sterile, and ready to go to work.

Woodie stood next to the patient, facing me. She said, "Clara, Dr. Davis is going to put a green cloth on your tummy to put the baby on when it's delivered. Just settle comfortably, m'dear. We're nearly there."

I laid it neatly as I could, taking care not to touch Clara's legs.

"He's just going to examine you to make sure that the cervix is well out of the way."

When I put the fingers of my right hand into the vagina I could feel how closely the baby's head was applied. It was surprising that Clara could not push it that bit further into our world. I took my hand out. There was a strong smell of meconium. What little I saw of that liquid was not dark green, which was a good thing.

"Now," said Woodie, "he's going to make sure the blades of the forceps are clean."

I picked up the Wrigley's and dunked them in a stainless-steel bowl of sterile liquid. I had forgotten how small the handle was, compared with other forceps such as the Kiellands. I separated the two halves.

"Left side first. Dr. Davis is going to put that blade in. You'll likely feel his hand on that side, inside you."

I followed instructions. Like all forceps, the spoon-shaped blades of the Wrigley's were curved to encompass the baby's head without crushing it. Where the belly of the spoon would have been was an open space, the size of a small palm. The blade that curved to the baby's left was curved to my right, but its half of the handle lay in my left hand. I slipped my right hand into the space between the child's head and vaginal wall. Then I slid the blade along my palm. The liquid in which I had washed the metal acted as a lubricant.

"He's making sure he doesn't trap the kiddie's ear with the blade," said Woodie. She grinned at me as I felt around as best I could. The tiny, soft ear was within the open space of the forceps' blade. I took my hand out and let the blade rest. The handle lowered a tiny bit.

"Now he's going to do the same on the other side." Woodie spoke quietly.

I slid the blade along my left palm. Again, I made sure the ear was not trapped under the smooth metal. Like the ear on the other side, it lay in the open space within the rim.

"Dr. Davis is going to make very sure that the two halves of the handle fit together without any effort, without him having to squeeze too much. That's how he'll know that the forceps are safely in place."

The gently ridged metal halves each had a straight inner edge.

I took a deep breath and pushed these two edges together. There was no real resistance which meant that the blades were cupping the head and not crushing it. I felt sweat trickling down my back. I nodded to Woodie.

"I've got to do an episiotomy, Mrs. Cawl," I said.

"You'll feel a cold sensation where the anaesthetic goes in, on the right side of your bum," said Woodie. She handed me the long needle. I pushed it in, down and outward from my position, through the muscle and fat. Mrs. Cawl moaned.

"Not much longer," said Woodie as she handed me the scissors. "Dr. Davis will cut so that when baby's head comes out it won't tear anything."

"Just get on with it, for Christ's sake!" said Mrs. Cawl.

Woodie leaned over and with her index finger traced a line from the lowest part of the vaginal opening to the right, into the buttock. I cut along the line to ensure that the two thick muscles of the anal ring that lay nearby would not be damaged during the next steps in the delivery. Making the incision was not as easy as I expected, though the tissues had been stretched tight as could be. They sprang apart as the scissors did their work. Small yellow pearls of fat glistened. Blood ran down and onto the thin, brown, rubber mat.

"Now Dr. Davis is going to pull the baby's head down and out, then up to deliver the baby's body, and you'll feel much, much, better."

I followed Woodie's directions. The forceps' handle fitted easily in my right hand as I grasped it from below. I clasped my left over the top of my right and pulled downward. It took far more effort than I expected. I pulled hard. I remembered the time I'd seen a registrar put his foot against the table to give himself more leverage as he used forceps to deliver a baby.

"Firmly," said Woodie. I pulled harder.

The baby's head crowned as Mrs. Cawl shouted, "Oh!"

Woodie leaned over to make sure the cord was not around its neck. I slipped the forceps off. There were no marks on the skin that covered the baby's skull. I smiled at Woodie. She smiled back and clapped her hands softly.

"All over but the shouting, Clara," she said to Mrs. Cawl. "Baby's fine. Dr. Davis has done his usual good job."

I sutured the episiotomy with catgut sutures. I was not going to do even that. At med school I'd been taught that any but the deepest episiotomy would heal well by itself as long as it was kept clean, but Woodie said, "You'd better stitch it up well. Mr. Cooper's a devil for that."

"What do you mean?"

"You'll see." She would not elaborate.

AFTERWARD WOODIE AND I SAT IN THE change room together, sipping black tea.

"I owe you," I said. I felt a million feet tall. I had conquered the world.

"From the smile on your face, you certainly do," Woodie said. "And I'll collect when the time comes, you can be sure."

"What's a middenrammer?"

"A dustman. In the US they call them garbagemen."

"How do you know that?"

"I had a Yankee boyfriend, once."

"A long time ago?"

"Yes."

"Go on…"

"I'll tell you my life story some other time," she said, "over the beer you owe me."

"How do you know her? Mrs. Cawl, I mean." I asked.

"She and I were talking about the men who own the fishing

boats and everything else around here. Her husband works for an owner my husband also worked for, as a trawlerman."

"What's does your husband do now, then?"

Woodie said, grimly, "Nowt. He's dead."

"I'm sorry. I didn't mean to pry..."

"Don't worry, Brian. You weren't to know." She stood up and threw the dregs of her tea in the sink. "Don't forget, you owe me a drink."

"No, I won't."

She smiled. "Maybe more than one."

LATER, WHEN ARJUN APPEARED to take my place, I found that I had lost all sense of time. The Delivery Suite had its own rhythm.

I was surprised to find it was evening outside. The rough grass at the edge of the path to the prefabs was wet. Perhaps it had rained. Perhaps it was just sea spray. The standard lamps along the way had a stippled halo around their bulbs. Everything looked washed and worn, and I felt the same.

ARJUN KNOCKED ON MY DOOR. "Time for rounds... Cooper's back ... We can't be late... C'mon!" His shirt was crisp, his tie Windsored, and the collar of his white coat turned up. Army-like, his shoes were polished, and there was a knife-edge to his trousers.

We walked through a cool mist that lay on the ground like a fallen cloud. Through the swirl, I could see hospital roof, but not the main doors. My face was warmed by the sun.

"She'll be in top form today," said Arjun.

"Who?"

"Corrigan. The Sister in charge of Ward One, where the post-deliveries and surgicals stay till they're fit to go home."

"What do you mean by 'top form'?" I asked.

"Some things are better experienced than described, my boy." He skipped a couple of times as we walked. "Like Woodie's temper. You run into it yet?"

"No," I said, as we joined Tripti at the front door.

"You'd better turn down that collar," he said. "We don't want Cooper to have a stroke on his first day back."

"Speak for yourself," said Arjun.

"No respect. This cannot be!" When Tripti curled his lip in a smile his black mustache bunched up over his white teeth.

Arjun stopped in front of a window to check his reflection. He turned down the coat collar and swung from side to side to ensure that it lay smoothly.

I looked to my right. In a small room with a large window, cigarette in hand, George sat at a bank of phone plugs. Earphones clung to his head and a curved black microphone dangled in front of his mouth. There were broad nicotine marks on his index and third fingers.

He grinned at me. "He's not in yet," he said, loudly. And then, into the microphone, "SweportMaternityhowcanIhelpyou? Right you are. Just a moment, please." He plugged a jack into one of the sockets in front of him. Sprawling back he said with a smile, "Off you go, gentlemen. There's still time to repent."

Tripti turned and led us through a pair of swing doors with small longitudinal windows at head height above scratched, grey-metal facing. The National Health Service must have bought a mountain of those same doors — I had bumped beds through them in every hospital I'd been in. One of the doors hit me on the upper arm as we went through.

The ward had fifteen beds down each side. Around each bed hung the usual pale blue-grey patterned curtains, drawn to create the illusion of privacy when examining a patient. Who's kidding who? There are few secrets in a hospital. In the middle, four extra beds had been squeezed in for acute cases that had to be admitted no matter what; three women in those beds made for a very tight fit of people and equipment. The fourth bed had been stripped down to a mattress and the brown, rubber sheet that covered it.

Of course, cramped conditions are not peculiar to small hospitals. An older, smoking, whisky-drinking friend of mine had developed cancer of the tongue and endured one of those savage operations that cure and mutilate at the same time. I went to visit her in the Royal National Throat, Nose and Ear Hospital in Central London, where she lay in a bed trying not to die. That ward, in an institute famous enough to get the Royal nod, was as crowded as any I had ever seen. Her bed was jammed-up against another, which had a man in it. If they'd rolled the wrong way they'd have risked arrest for indecency.

Ward One in Sweport was cut from the same cost-saving cloth. Management everywhere lives by the mantra, "Look, a free inch. Use it." For the next year only the people I worked with could make such crowded conditions tolerable.

Besides thirty-four beds, Sister Corrigan's ward held her tiny office and a desk between two of the extra beds for us to write up our charts. Farther down the ward an old crone in a green overall carefully swept the floor under each bed. When she straightened up she was still bent in half. Osteoporosis had broken her back.

The door to the Sister's office opened.

"Good morning, Sister!" Arjun said loudly. "You look so well today!"

"Enough of that, Dr. Chakraborty! I'm Irish, and you are Indian..."

"Brahmin, Sister, Brahmin!"

"... but you're the one who has kissed the Blarney Stone. I have told you before and will tell you again, your flannery cuts no ice with me."

The woman who spoke was dressed, like all Sisters in those days, in dark-blue uniform punctuated by white collar and cuffs.

A starched apron lay off her bosom on which lay a large cross. Small, fat, four-square, she had the thick legs and balding head of a rugby forward.

She turned and looked at me with one of her eyes. The other pointed in a different direction. "Who is this?" she asked.

Tripti said, "Dr. Brian Davis, Sister."

I held out my hand. "Pleased to meet you, Sister."

Ignoring my hand, she sniffed, "At least your hair is properly cut. Not like the last one." With one walleye still staring in my direction, she clapped and shouted, "Nurse! That bed is not well-made. The bottom sheet is not properly folded at the corners, as you should well know by now. Strip it and make it again! You're a disgrace to your profession. And the rest of you… I'm coming round later. You'd better be ready! Everything had better be shipshape!"

Behind her a blushing nurse jumped to work. Corrigan wrinkled her chin. She was in charge, could see round corners and made sure all knew it. Folding her hands on her stomach she stared at me. "Dr. Mehta!" (It was Tripti she was addressing. He was six feet to my left) "Mr. Cooper called. He will be here in a wee while. He asked that you start rounds."

Tripti said, in a deferential tone, "Thank you, Sister."

What was the matter with everyone? Why did they kowtow to this petty tyrant?

"I did not appreciate your comment about my hair, Sister," I said. "How I grow it is my business and not yours."

There was a dead silence. Corrigan straightened her back.

"Dr. Mehta, I will wait in my office till Mr. Cooper comes," she said. "Staff will go with you." She jerked her head and Staff, in a lighter-blue uniform, scuttled over.

"Oh boy!" Arjun whispered as her door closed.

"That old battleaxe will not ride roughshod over me," I said.

Arjun clapped me on the back, "Clearly!"

"She can see through the curtains," said Tripti.

I shrugged.

We went to the end of the ward and started the daily rounds.

The first patient lay on her side, the blankets barely covering her lower half.

"I need to see your episiotomy," Tripti said to her. "Draw the curtains, Staff."

Privacy appeased, he pulled down the covers. "Roll over, please, on to your back."

"It's still sore," the woman said as she flapped her knees apart to show her perineum.

"What's that?" I blurted. A wad of dark-blue plastic thread, tied in a convoluted lump, lay at the end of an episiotomy scar.

"It bleddy hurts, whatever it is," the woman said.

"This is a Dr. Cooper special," said Arjun.

"That's nylon thread, isn't it?" I said. "What the hell for?"

"It's the way Dr. Cooper sutures episiotomies."

"But those stitches will never dissolve!"

"He takes the sutures out at the end of a week," Arjun said. "It is his way."

I looked more closely. There were several stitches, each individually tied, with long ends that themselves had been tied together in a large knot.

The patient saw my expression. She grunted, closed her legs and said, "It's like sitting on a bunch of thistles and it bleddy hurts. He's a bugger, that one. I wanted the other old man, but he's took sick just when I need him. He don't stitch hairbrushes onto your fanny."

Staff choked on a laugh. We moved away from the patient.

"Don't look gobsmacked, Brian," said Arjun. "This is only a small part of what goes on here. There's more to come. We are in a misogynist's playground."

"Rubbish!" said Tripti. "Dr. Cooper's methods work. His episiotomies heal well. That's what counts."

"Rubbish it is not!" said Arjun. "I'm telling the God's truth. He hates women. Why else would he suture them that way? And, remember, it's only a couple of weeks since you ran like mad to do a Caesar to prevent him from putting on midforceps and tearing the woman's insides to pieces. No one in the Western world does those any more, but he does. Use a ventouse suction extractor like they use all over now? He'd rather chop off his hands. 'Why make it easy on the woman?' is his mantra."

Tripti's pager beeped, and he went to the phone. Staff followed him.

The patient got out of bed and walked gingerly to French windows leading to a balcony, a pack of cigarettes and a box of Swan Vestas in her hand — she was the woman I had seen my first evening, smoking while attached to a drip.

I said to Arjun, "It's ridiculous. Nylon is rarely used for skin, and I've never seen it used for an episiotomy. Why does Tripti defend it? He must know better."

Arjun leaned against the foot of the patient's bed and swung his Littmann stethoscope around his neck, Yankee style. "He won't cross Cooper because of what happened in Uganda. He's frightened of anything that threatens the rule of law. If the status quo is working, and he and his are not being harmed, he'll support it."

"What happened to them?"

"I don't know what happened to *them,* but Sunita once told me about something that happened to Tripti in the casino." Arjun seemed to have no qualms about revealing the confidence.

"There are casinos in Uganda?"

"Of course, my dear chap. In Kampala, at least. There are casinos in every large African city. Anyway, it turns out that

Tripti was a big gambler. His family had made stacks of money —
through trade, buying and selling land, that kind of thing at
which we're so good. We Indians," he added, in case it had not
been clear. He smiled, and went on. "The Brits made sure we
were transported all over the Empire from Mother India to run
things properly, and we did. We still do. We're doing it in the UK
now." He straightened his cuffs and said, "Tripti was in the habit
of going to the casinos. Sunita knew they were full of prossies,
but he promised her he wasn't doing anything with any of them.
She elected to believe him. Who knows why... another man's
marriage... best of a bad job... whatever." He shrugged. "Well
one day, out of the blue — if we are to believe what we are told —
one of the girls accused Tripti of something, God knows why.
The upshot was that he was badly beaten."

Warm air blew in through the open French windows, and with
it the smell of the sea. I heard the sound of machinery. It came
close and then moved away, a boat going out to sea, taking its
whole world with it.

Arjun continued, "He won't talk about it. At least not to me."

"You asked him?"

"I was curious. I wanted to know. You don't ask, you don't get."

I knew then not to say anything to Arjun that I didn't want
the whole world to hear. He had made me curious, however. He
knew his audience. "How did Sunita find out?" I asked.

"He was in hospital for quite a few days. I suppose that's when.
Anyway, it was the start of a change for them. The beating really
shook his tree. So they emigrated, using their British passports,
to come to smelly Sweport of all places."

He grinned and said, "They're both making damn sure it's not
from frying pan to fire. She's into everything. Women's Institute,
good works: you ask, she volunteers. And him, he works all the
hours God made and then some."

"Why?"

"With Leander sick, if our registrar keeps his nose clean, Sweport Maternity-style, he'll get to be locum consultant. And it's onward and upward from there — 'cos no one in his right mind would want to work here forever."

Tripti and Staff reappeared. We walked to the next bed, but before we could get started an older, sandy-haired man appeared, small and bent slightly forward, but with a look of command bred-in-the-bone. It was Dr. Cooper.

Corrigan went to greet him and said something that made him give me a hard look.

Cooper walked to the bedside. Corrigan, Tripti, and Staff fell in behind him.

"Ah, Dr. Davis, our new, well-travelled addition to the team. You're here at last. Join on the end of the line, please." He had a low, determined voice with hardly a trace of a Yorkshire accent. After that he took no more notice of me until the end of the round.

We trailed along in the tried-and-true method developed over the years in hospitals such as Barts and Guys. At each bedside Cooper asked questions of Staff, flipped through the chart, laid on hands, dictated the next steps for that patient's care and occasionally even spoke to her. After we'd seen a couple of patients I knew that the pompous rigmarole was just like other hospitals I had worked in, only worse.

As we progressed it became clear that the habit of Mr. Cooper, FRCOG, was to descend from on high, only to give instructions. Whatever he ordered, Corrigan said, "Yes, Mr. Cooper" in a loud voice, even if he was talking to Tripti. At the end he turned to her and said, "The ward looks as shipshape as ever, Sister. It's a credit to you."

She rose on to her toes, blushed and said, "Thank you, Sir."

Cooper looked at me and said, "Come to dinner on Thursday, at my house, Dr. Davis. It is an indulgence of mine, a ritual for newcomers."

He clearly knew the staff schedule, and that this Thursday was my evening off. There was no doubt in his mind but that I would say yes. Not troubling himself to tell me where he lived, he added, "Dr. Chak will tell you where to find us. He's been."

I saw Woodie in the cafeteria at lunchtime. I was trying to decide if I should sit next to her or not when she stood up, tray in hand.

As she passed me she said, "Met Corrigan, didn't you?"

I nodded.

"Into every life a little rain must fall, Dr. Davis."

"I thought you were going to call me Brian."

"You're right," she said, a pleased smile on her face.

"Don't forget I owe you a drink," I said.

"I've not forgotten. I wouldn't, would I, not where a free drink is concerned?"

Watching her walk away I felt better than I had all morning.

EVERY BRANCH OF MEDICINE has a system. They all start with routine questions to be answered that set the stage and place the patient where she should be in the known hierarchy of likely diseases or potential problems. The first brush with an in-patient is known as clerking, and for the duration of my time at Sweport Maternity, that is what I did when on call.

My clerking routine there went like this:

Take the history: Did she have proper antenatal care? Did she go to antenatal classes? (Both of which give a good clue as to what's going to happen.) How much does she smoke, in case she needs an anaesthetic? How many kids has she had? Did those deliveries go off okay? What was the date of her last menstrual period? What's her past medical history?

Examine her: check blood pressure, weight for size, pulse. Any obvious defects in her skeleton; does she have an odd shape? How does her chest sound? Any heart murmurs? Is this one young or old for her age?

Do the internal: Cervix dilated? How many fingers? Is the baby's head floating free, or is it in the pelvis? Stick the trumpet on her belly to see what the baby's heart rate is — is it regular? Does the pelvis feel okay? (You measure front to back using, as a rough ruler, the distance from the tip of your third finger, along the back of your hand to the wrist.) Will she need an enema, and, if so, now or later?

And finally: What do you and the midwife think of her — that insensible moment of truth earned through experience — will this be a straightforward delivery? What's your gut feeling? Is she a calm one? If yes, it'll be easier; if no, only God knows, and he isn't telling till the last bloody moment.

Over and over, the same routine, till I could spot a problem even on two hours' kip, whether I was exhausted, happy, sad or preoccupied. Till that part of my mind could work independently of *me* in the practice of good medicine. Practice being the operative word. I once heard a family doc comment that by the time he retired after forty years of treating people, he had asked "What's the problem?" four hundred thousand times. You had better not get tired of asking questions.

WHEN THURSDAY EVENING CAME I took the bus that stopped outside the hospital.

"Hold yer tight!" the conductress shouted and then rang the bell. I liked the way she looked at me as she gave me my change and promised to tell me when we reached Cooper's street.

"G'night," I said as I got off.

"Hold yer tight!" she said and winked at me. A beauty of brevity.

It was a large, square, very old two-storey house with wooden gables, white-washed plaster walls, and a pebbled forecourt ringed by tall lilac bushes. Two cars were parked in front of a stable that had been converted into a garage. On its roof was a weather vane in the shape of a horse and rider wearing what looked like a Cavalier's hat.

The pebbles rustled and scraped as I walked to the front door. I rang the bell, but heard nothing. Finally a young boy appeared and opened it.

"Are you Dr. Davis?" he asked.

"Yes."

"I'm to take your coat."

"I'm not wearing one," I said. The house smelled of apples and something sweet.

"Oh... well... Come in please. This way. My dad said you're to wait in the study. Mum's getting supper ready, and he's washing up after the garden."

The panelled study was dominated by a large picture of the crucifixion set in an ornate gilt frame, leaning forward from the wall. Blood dripped down Christ's forehead from the crown of thorns. More drops of blood, deep red and reflecting light, fell from the shaft of a spear that was stuck between ribs on the body's right side. A weather-beaten Roman centurion stood below the crucified God, one hand upraised as if pushing the sight away, the other to his mouth. The perspective was wrong, the colours muted, the sky above Golgotha hidden by dark cloud. But the painting had presence.

"He is the first soldier of Christ. He converted to Christianity from the Mithraic bull-sacrificing tradition that most Roman soldiers followed," said Cooper. I had not heard him come in. "He was paid to stick the spear in, to shorten the time to death."

"What do you mean?"

"It was common practice for relatives to pay a soldier to spear a crucified man between the ribs so that he would die more quickly. I am sure a collapsed lung would do just that... truncate the man's suffering. The Romans used this punishment so

much that they would know full well how to shorten the pain...
or how to amplify it, come to that, usually by crucifying a man
upside down, which is what they did to traitors.

He went over to the picture and flicked a speck of dust off the
frame as he continued, "Spearing our Lord changed this centurion's life. This ignorant soldier, this brute, was so moved by the
devotion of His followers, and by the rainstorm that beat down
upon them, as is forecast by the clouds in this painting, that he
converted to Christianity. He said it was because even the heav-
ens cried. I believe that to be the truth."

"How do you know all this?"

"I study the Bible and its historical basis. It is of paramount
importance to me." After a pause, he said, "I live according to
the precepts of the Church. I make a point of understanding the
relevance of Christianity to modern-day life." He had no guile. He
said, "I believe with all my heart and with all my soul. Perhaps
you will come to that one day."

I said nothing. Clearly he had heard I was not a believer. Had
he also heard of my years among the student radicals of Paris and
Berlin? At any rate, least said, soonest mended; I did not want to
argue with a man who believed so deeply. I had been through that
with David, my radical friend, and come off the worse for it each
time.

The meal was a surprise. Its tone was set by the boy, the older
of two, who said Grace in a firm voice. "For what we are about to
receive, may the Lord make us truly thankful. Make us whole
for thee."

"Matthew, tell Dr. Davis where else that Grace was said," his
father ordered.

His wife was a good deal younger than Cooper. "Oh dear," she
said. "Not again."

"No, Trudy, I'm sure Dr. Davis will find it interesting."

The boy said, "In Nelson's day, battleships used to sail past each other firing broadside after broadside. Each sailor knew that he might well die and wanted to have God's blessing, just in case. So just before English ships were to be fired upon, the youngest midshipman would stand on the quarterdeck and say Grace."

"Then it should have been me to say Grace," the other boy said. "I'm the youngest."

"This isn't a battle, stupid," said Matthew.

"Matthew!" said their mother, then, "Next time, Mark."

"Anyway, what happened to *Benedictus benedicat?*" Mark asked. "That's what we usually say."

"We have a guest," said Cooper. "The longer Grace was warranted."

The dining room walls were painted a rich red, the window frames white, and the fitted carpet a very dark green. Everything in the room appeared carefully thought out. A silver salt cellar sat on the mahogany table, in the shape of an eighteenth-century ship of the line, its sails billowing. It was nearer Cooper and his sons than his wife, who sat opposite him. I was below the salt.

He saw me looking at the silver ship. "Striking, isn't it? My family has been sailors from Viking times. This area was invaded and then settled by Norsemen in the centuries before the Dark Ages. That's why there are so many tall, raw-boned, fair-haired people around here."

"Raw-boned and hard-headed," said his wife. She was smiling.

"Trudy is from Liverpool. They are quite unlike us. They speak differently."

I hadn't noticed that she had an accent much different from his. What I did notice was how confident the four of them were.

I'd expected fish, given that we were in a seaport, but dinner was roast beef and Yorkshire pudding, the meat cut so thin you could see through it, in the upper-class English fashion. It lay on my plate alongside well-cooked vegetables.

The main items on the menu, however, were politics and religion.

"I hear you were in Paris during the student riots," said Trudy.

"Yes."

"Why?"

"For me, then, it was the right thing to do, the right place to be."

"Our church has a discussion group that meets once a month. Would you come and give them a talk about your experience, what happened there, why you went? It seems such an unusual thing to do."

I said, "I'd have to think about that. I'm not a good public speaker." The last thing I wanted was to explain myself to a church group.

Matthew said, "May we leave the table, please?"

"Yes," said his father.

"It's my turn!" shouted Mark. He reached across, picked up the salt cellar and took it across to a bow-fronted credenza. "C'mon Matthew!" he said. "You know I need your help." He was holding the boat with both hands. I saw that there was a large cross on its mainsail, silver standing proud of silver. In real life it would have been in scarlet and the height and breadth of three men. His brother opened one of the curved glass side doors and, with great care, Mark put the ornate carving on a shelf. The two boys ran out of the room.

"If you believe in something enough, then the passion will come through and the reasons be clear, no matter how badly you think you speak," said Cooper, pulling my attention back.

"Yes, exactly," said Trudy. She leaned forward, pushing her hair behind her ears. I could hear the boys shouting somewhere.

She said, "I'm no student radical, but I feel I can relate to people who *commit* to something. Just as I'm committed — as *we're* committed," she corrected herself, glancing toward Cooper.

"To what?" I asked.

"We believe that abortion is wrong." She stared at me — was it to judge my reaction? "We *know* it is."

Her husband chimed in. "And we *know* that the Church's teachings on this matter are right."

"And I, *we*, will do whatever it takes to enact those teachings," Trudy said vehemently. Changed by passion, her face looked older, and his looked younger.

Again "I" changed quickly to "we." Was she the driving force in the relationship? Many of the married women who had marched with us in Paris had been like that. They had to be; their men had accepted the status quo while they no longer could. They led, their men followed.

Cooper stood up. "You may have heard that the opportunity has arisen to stop abortions being carried out at our hospital."

"No," I said. "I've been busy finding my feet doing deliveries. According to the rotation I'm not involved in elective surgeries for another month."

"Abortions are never elective for the baby," said Trudy. "How could they be?"

"Dr. Leander stood in our way," said Cooper.

"Is he coming back?" I asked.

"No, unfortunately he's too sick to continue working."

"There's nothing unfortunate about it," said his wife. "Now, finally, we can set things straight."

Somewhere above I heard the boys shouting. Something fell with a thud, and one of them yelled, "Watch it, looney!"

Trudy took no notice. She leaned forward and said, "How can we go on allowing mothers to murder their babies? And the doctors who perform abortions? Middenrammers! Clearing away women's failures like the leavings of a bad meal."

Cooper smiled, proud of her.

She inclined her head toward me and raised one eyebrow.

"Who is not for us, is against us," Cooper said, looking directly at me.

Berlin had taught me the best way to cope with threats. I shrugged. His face reddened. His wife sat back. Then she got up and walked out of the room.

As I was leaving, Cooper said, "I want you to see this."

In the hallway he stopped by a wood panel and pressed one of its sides. The panel swung open to reveal a small chamber in which there was a seat set in the wall facing a cross set above a shelf with two candlesticks.

"When Elizabeth I rounded up Catholic priests my ancestors sheltered one. For months he hid here whenever the soldiers came by. I pride myself that I would do the same."

He closed the door. "I'd like your help to put some boxes in my car." It was more of a demand than a request.

We loaded six letter-sized cardboard boxes, long and heavy. As I hefted each one I felt my gorge rising. He and his wife had presented me with a stark choice in a crude attempt to abrogate my free will.

He said, "They're record sheets for Mr. Burke. I've had them printed for him. Our hospital manager is a stickler for detailed information. There is a change. I'll show you." He took out two sheets. "This is the old one... See the headings: *TOPDAM*... *Terminations of Pregnancy, Delivery route, Abortion, Miscarriage* ... Now look at the new one we've had made. See? *TOPDM*. After the Board has its next meeting we will no longer be recording the number of abortions. There will have been none."

He tore the old sheet into several pieces, with a flourish.

"What do you think?" He was giving me another chance to redeem myself. "It's an improvement, isn't it?" He was softer than his wife, who had not come to see me off.

I said, "I've no idea." To test the wind, I asked him for a lift to the hospital.

"I'm sorry, Dr. Davis, I have much paperwork to do." He looked at his watch and said, "There'll be a bus in a few minutes."

I had not agreed to speak to the church group, nor voiced any agreement with them about abortion, nor commented on the form. I would be taking the bus.

ARJUN TRAPPED ME in the common room next morning. As usual, his trouser creases were perfect. He had no wife, and though he clearly had money I had not seen anyone hired to help him. He was a dandy of determination, then, prepared to work for his cause.

"How was your dinner?" he said.

"Weird," I said.

"She's a pip, isn't she? Hard to take. And what she says about abortion—I can't believe a woman would think that way nowadays. It's 1970—not 1917!"

"She's committed... They're both committed, I'll say that for them."

"They need committing," he said. "They've all but put an end to abortions at Sweport Maternity. The manager, Burke, and the Board have only to rubber stamp it, and they will. The Coopers will start on the outpatient birth control clinic next. It's back to the Middle Ages, and damn the women of Sweport. How the hell I ended up here I'll never know. Thank God I've another job lined up in a civilized place. I've only got to last another few months."

"Where are you going?"

"Bradford."

"Civilized?"

"It is from where I sit right now." He paused for a moment. Did they ask you to give a talk to their church group?"

"Yes."

"When are you doing it?"

"I didn't say I would. Did they ask you?"

"Yes. They wanted me to talk about being a Brahmin."

"And you did?"

"Yes." He straightened his cuffs. "Not one of my best moments. I felt like a specimen under glass. Will you go to speak?"

"No."

"What excuse will you give?"

"If he asks me again I'll just refuse."

"He'll hold it against you."

"Sod him," I said. I didn't care what Cooper thought, or whether it would affect my chances of getting a good reference and a better job, in Bradford or anywhere else. Arjun looked as if he wished he could afford to feel the same way.

Of course dinner at the Coopers' was fodder for conversation elsewhere, as well. Talking to Sheila in the doctors' common room, I said, "Cooper and his wife are so self-assured. So are their kids. It's impressive."

"That's what having faith does for you. Gives you an extra leg to stand on. Helps your emotional balance, at least they think it does. Me, I have my music." She ran her fingers up and down her forearm again, practicing runs. I could hear the faint slap of skin upon skin as she said, "What about you? What do you have?"

It was the same question David had asked me in our last argument before he went to back to Germany with Cohn-Bendit and the other radicals, and I went back to England. I still didn't have an answer.

ONE NIGHT I WENT TO the instrument cupboard outside the small O.R. kitty-corner to Ward One.

"Can I help you?" said Jessie the midwife, who appeared beside me.

"I want to see a curette, one used in a D. and C.," I said.

She stared for a moment, then reached into the cupboard and produced a long, thin package covered in the rough brown paper. The striped sealing tape had turned the blue-grey, which showed it had been through the sterilizer.

"We'll not be using these very often now," she said. "Thank God."

"So I understand."

I sat on a windowsill and opened the package. I had used an instrument like this during training when scrubbed for an O.R. list, which started, as usual, with a D. and C. to remove abnormal tissue from the uterus. When my tutor put the curette in my hand I'd been struck by its resemblance to the spoons used for ice cream sundaes, the ones served in tall glasses with ice cream in the middle and fruit smeared against the sides. In the curette, the belly of the spoon's bowl had been removed and both edges of the remaining metal rim sharpened.

"Be careful with it," he'd told me. "You don't want to go through her vaginal walls."

Very gingerly I had slipped the curette through the cervical os until it came up against something solid.

"Now scrape it back and forth, but gently."

I did that a few times. It felt like coring out the inside of an overripe grapefruit. The pulp was the endometrium that lined the womb, and the fruit's hard skin the muscle of the uterine wall. There was a gritty feel to each stroke.

"Let me finish. We've got the whole list to get through," my boss had said.

At the end of the short procedure the contents of the curettage, small red and maroon lumps of bloody material, lay in a stainless-steel kidney bowl. It was easy to imagine how an early foetus, which resembles a cashew nut in shape and size but with tiny limb buds, would have looked in among the curettings.

IN MED SCHOOL we were taught that a doctor should not spend time looking for the unexpected. "Common things are common" is the aphorism. However, there are exceptions to every rule.

One day, a few months after I'd arrived in Sweport, a patient arrived in early labour. All was routine, until I put my gloved hand into her vagina to see how far her cervix was dilated. Something warm, firm, and pulsating slipped into my palm. I took a moment to go through the possibilities. It could not be an oddly elongated cervix. I'd felt one of those a couple of days before and, though quite firm and round, it had not pulsated. Whatever this was it could not be vaginal wall curled round in some weird way. It was too solid and discrete for that. With a shock I realized I had the umbilical cord in my hand. It had prolapsed through the cervix and come to lie in front of the baby's head.

Passages from my favourite textbook, Donald's *Practical Obstetric Problems*, ran through my mind. I knew I had to prevent the descending head squeezing the cord during the final stage of delivery or it would cut off the child's oxygen supply just minutes before tiny lungs could take over. The result would be a stillbirth at term.

"Get Tripti here," I said.

"Why?" asked the midwife.

"Just do it," I hissed.

She shot me a look, but she went.

Tripti arrived, irritated. "What is the problem?"

I whispered, "I've got the cord in my hand."

"Don't talk nonsense," he said.

"See for yourself."

"Don't move," he said and put a glove on his right hand.

"How do we do this?" I asked.

"You're so green," he said. He leaned over and slipped his hand inside mine so that the back of his hand lay against my palm. We were as close as twins in utero, he leaning right on me. I felt his fingers moving along the pulsating object. There was a faint, pleasant smell of curry mixed with aftershave.

"You're right," he said. "I can't believe it."

He took his hand out and stood upright. After a moment he said, "This is as rare as hen's teeth. Whatever you do don't take your hand out. You can't let the head come down on that cord. Push back if you have to." And then, "At least she's early on."

He turned round and said in a loud voice, "My dear, there is a problem. The cord is in the wrong place, and to make sure the baby will be okay we have to do an immediate Caesarian section."

The patient's answer was to let out a loud sob and then a cry. I saw her stomach bunch up as the uterus contracted and, at the same moment, felt the baby's head come barrelling down on my braced fingers. It was as if someone was ramming a bowling ball against them, as hard as could be. I managed to prevent the cord being crushed, but sweat broke out on my forehead as I pushed back. I had not realized how strongly a uterus contracts in full labour.

"O.R. One is being cleaned," said Tripti. "We'll do it in O.R. Two. I'll get things going." He smiled at the patient and said to me, quietly, "She has to be brought down right away, and you can't let that head through so keep your hand in there till she's delivered. We're counting on you." I heard him say to the midwife, "Get George up here with a stretcher. Let's get a move on."

By the time George appeared I had fought off the baby's head four times. I calculated the patient was contracting every two and half minutes. At each contraction I arched my fingers and pushed back. The muscles in my arm hurt.

"Sorry I'm so slow. It's visiting hours, and the lift is being used by relatives. God forbid they should climb a few flights," George said. He lined the stretcher up by the bed and said, "Okay, m'dear, you've got to slide over onto here so we can take you downstairs."

"I can't take my hand out," I said. "The cord mustn't get crushed by the baby's head. She's in full labour."

George took a second and then said, "You'd better climb up on there with her because that's the only way I can move the both of you together."

That was how I found myself on a narrow stretcher crouching between a patient's legs, my hand in her vagina, with a blanket covering her lower half and most of my right arm. It took both George and the nurse to push us into the corridor.

"Christ!" he said, "you're heavy."

"You cheeky sod," the patient said, then, "Oh, Oh! Oh bleddy hell, it hurts!"

I grunted in reply as I pushed back at the head. My arm was sore, and my fingers had become numb. I was sweating as much as the woman lying in front of me. My back started to ache.

The lift was surrounded by relatives since it was the end of visiting hours. George had to say, "Let us through, please!" a couple of times before they made way for us. One even opened the gates. The patient gave a yelp as we jerked over the lip of the lift floor and someone said, "Oh!"

My back was to the corridor when we came to rest. To my astonishment most of the relatives piled in, surrounding us.

"Press ground!" the nurse said. On the way down no one looked me in the eye. This was England, after all. There was complete silence, except for the woman's cries as her uterus contracted. I pushed as hard as I could against the bowling ball and heard myself grunt in harmony with the old machinery. It was a musical trip at the end of which my hand and arm were numb.

When we reached the ground floor there was a mad scramble by the onlookers to get out, leaving us behind.

"Thank God!" said George. He pushed with one leg against the back of the lift and got us moving. Once in the corridor he turned the stretcher sharp left toward Ward One. He said to the nurse, "Go on, lass, hurry up. Open those doors." And then Corrigan appeared.

"You're not coming through here," she said, standing with her arms crossed.

"What d'you mean?" said George, and the stretcher ground to a halt.

"Hospital regulations forbid a patient in labour going through the post-op ward, for fear of infection."

"Don't talk daft," George said.

"Don't you talk to me like that!" she shot back.

He said, "I've got to get her to the O.R. right quick. She's to have a Caesar, the sooner the better. To stop the head..."

"I understand what's happening," Corrigan said, "but a rule is there for a purpose."

"Sister," I said. "You can't be serious. Let us through."

"No." She was firm. She pointed at the doors to the parking lot, "Go across the quadrangle."

"What?" I shouted. "Outside?"

"Exactly," she said. "And don't you shout at me. I'm doing what's right."

"Oh, oh, please hurry! For the love of God!" yelled the patient.

"Jesus wept!" said George. He swung the stretcher round and pushed it through the front doors.

"There's no need to swear," I heard Corrigan say as the doors closed.

I would have said something in reply, but was too busy keeping my balance as we bounced across wet cobbles. I could not believe what was happening. Visitors' cars drove slowly past in the rain. I heard the slap of windscreen wipers and the slurry of rubber on stone.

We reached the back doors of O.R. Two. The nurse banged hard on them. An orderly in greens pushed them open. George said, "Give us a hand, lad," and we were in.

"Over here, double-quick!" said Tripti. "Let's get this baby out."

The stretcher was lined up next to the O.R. table. The patient and I slid over, its thick, black, rubber mattress cushioning the move. I could see my reflection, crouched and bent over, in the metal sides of the instrument trolley.

Tripti, Sheila, and Woodie were gowned up, their greens in sharp contrast to the white and black of the O.R. The anaesthetist on call, a thin balding Scotsman, put down the *Times* crossword he had been doing and said, "What is this caravanserai you've brought me, Tripti?"

"Just gas her!" Tripti said fiercely.

"Pfannenstiel?" asked Woodie.

"Yes!" said Tripti and held out his hand. "Scalpel! Let's get a move on!"

A whiff of anaesthetic, and the patient went lax, but her uterus did not. My arm and hand were no longer a part of me. My head was swimming, and my body was stiff from being bent over between the patient's legs.

There was a flash of light off the scalpel blade. Skin parted in a long, smiling curve. I saw muscle cut, peritoneum tented by tweezers, then pierced to reveal the bulging uterus.

There was a moment's silence and then Tripti said, "Cutting the uterus. Sheila, get suction ready for the baby's mouth!"

"I know," she said. "We've been here before."

Two minutes later Tripti pulled the baby out through the incision, a gaping grin at the lowest part of its mother's stomach. The child yelled at the top of its lungs, after Sheila had cleared its mouth and as it felt cold air.

I could not move. My stiff arm, not under my control, stuck up through the abdominal wall.

Sheila leaned over, pulled off a glove and shook my hand.

"Good work," she said.

"You're contaminated now," said Woodie.

"I'll regown," said Sheila. "I couldn't resist."

Next morning there was a bottle of whisky on my front step with a note saying, "Thank you for your expertise and help." It was signed by a Mrs. Staples.

"She's the mother of the woman you had your hand inside for so long," said Arjun, who knew everything. "Very well-connected, she is."

My hand was stiff for several days. Long linear bruises stretched from between my fingers to my elbow. But I was happy. Mother and child were perfectly well.

9

I HAD THE WEEKEND OFF, but nowhere to go. My fingers ached. I was lonely. I remembered Paris and, before that, Berlin; the memories did not help. My life now centred round the Delivery Suite. When I was there life was technicoloured, urgent, fulfilling; outside of it there was nothing of any importance. I was unbalanced, like a soldier in a distant war, cut off from home, but needed where he was.

I had to deal with a never-ending stream of deliveries. The babies themselves were not a problem. Lurking in the background was the disquieting knowledge that the unexpected could turn a routine birth into a memorably explosive one, as had just happened. With nothing to do but worry I thought *sod it,* and I fell asleep watching the television.

The phone woke me on Saturday morning. Someone said, "Dost tha want summat nice for tha tea, lad?"

The accent was such broad Yorkshire that for a moment I was flummoxed. "What?"

"You owe me a beer." It was Woodie. "What about supper with it? You buy the booze, we go Dutch on the food."

"Okay. Where?" I was suddenly all ears.

"Take the bus into town so's you get there at five. I'll meet you at the stop outside the Grand."

There was no question about it. She more than interested me.

The bus conductor, a different one from last time, said, "Hold yer tight!" The bus trundled past the back of the hospital, and I could see my prefab between the houses we passed, through the trees and across the common.

Tripti would be working, as usual. His kids were out playing; I could not see Sunita or anyone else. Arjun was off chasing nurses again, hoping his new car would bring him luck. The little Brahmin had money, and that, coupled with his eternal good humour, gave him the sort of success he seemed to crave. "Dynamite comes in small bundles!" he would say with a wink after a night out.

For once there were no lying-in patients. I guessed that Sheila, whose weekend on call it was, was practicing, though I had not heard her violin before I left. She might have put a mute on its bridge to dull the sound, but I knew she did not like to use one. "It's like a singer practicing with a hoarse voice," I had heard her say.

It was a warm night. The girls on the bus wore loose blouses and had beehive hairstyles. I wondered what Woodie was wearing.

I stood outside the Grand for only a moment before Woodie appeared, driving an old Ford Popular. She leaned over and opened the passenger door.

"Get in," she said. "I didn't want to collect you from the hospital."

I did not need to ask why. Hospitals are gossip factories. I climbed in, remembering the cramped front of these old Ford

Pops as my feet wedged themselves between the gear box and the wheel arch. As the car pulled out I looked to see if there was an illuminated orange indicator arm sticking out of the central panel between the doors. There was not. The car was not that old, then, but you would not have known from the noises it made.

Woodie said, "I want you to tell me about Paris, how you got there... *why* you went."

"Why do you want to know?"

Instead of answering directly she said, "Have you ever seen inside a trawler?"

"No."

"Would you like to?"

"Yes.

"Let's go for a beer. Then after you've told me about Paris, I'll do both explaining and showing... maybe." There was no point in trying to push Woodie to do anything she did not want to do. It was not what she said, but how she said it. The kindest description would be "determined." If, after getting to know me, she did not want to show me the inside of a trawler, she would not.

I didn't care. I was happy to be alone with her.

We talked about Sweport as we drove through a tree-lined part of the town. The semi-detached houses, many with dormer windows, were neatly painted. Most cars in the driveways were Morris 1100s, those wide, squat, cartoon cars that threatened no one. The flower beds were well-tended. I said so.

"Everyone around here is law-abiding," she said. "And everything around here is safe. But you'll be wanting to see the real Sweport, Brian."

We left that part of town and turned toward the sea as it grew dark. Row houses, jammed one against the other, lined streets that ran down toward the shore, separated from it by a wall behind which was a laneway used only by sailors and fishermen.

Our forearms had touched as we turned a corner. Everything glistened in the fading light, dampened by windblown spray. But we were warm and dry in the car, cocooned against the world.

We followed the road as it swung over a hill and crossed to the spit of land which formed one side of the port's natural harbour. The grass verge grew more unkempt, and trees brushed the car's roof. Through my window I saw distant lights across the water. The road became rougher. We bounced along, finally reaching a gravel-filled car park in front of a long, low, well-lit building. Weathered picnic tables stood on a concrete landing that led to the water. A large sign proclaimed that it was a "Free Pub."

"Here we are," Woodie said. When she turned off the ignition the engine shuddered to a stop. The long gear stick, with its polished black nob, shook noisily. We sat for a moment.

"The timing needs adjusting," I said.

"This car was Joe's," she said. "Since he died nothing gets done to it."

Once inside we looked this way and that for an empty table. Her hair was in a knot on the top of her head and wisps of it hung down around her neck. I was conscious of the rise and fall of her breasts as she breathed. The pub was crowded. Everyone knew her. I caught people staring at me. The publican shouted, "Hello lass, tha table's in't booth, there!"

We sat facing each other. A waitress came over.

"Hello, luv," she said to Woodie. "What'll you have?"

"Cod and chips, and a pint of bitter. Brian, you should have the Dover sole."

"Right," I said. "And make it two pints."

"Tell me about Paris," Woodie said when the waitress left. "Why did you go there?"

"I went to Berlin first," I said. A plate dropped in the kitchen, and somebody screamed, the sounds shattering the air. We both turned round. Turning back I said, "We were going to change the world for the better."

"I understand wanting that," she said with feeling. "Who's 'we'?"

The beer arrived. The waitress stood the glasses on mats with a picture of a bull on them. Woodie took a drink.

"I went with David, a friend from medical school," I said.

"How come?"

"He preached revolution, I listened. He put into words what I felt, what I *believed*."

"And that was?" she asked, looking at me closely, her head bent forward.

"We knew in our hearts that the world is run unfairly, and that we could do something about it. All we had to do, all of us who gathered in Berlin and Paris, was to persist. We believed the time was right, that we were needed."

"Go on," she said quietly. "What did you do when you got there?"

"Talked, talked, and talked some more — then when we were wound up enough we scrawled graffiti on walls, heckled politicians, scattered pamphlets everywhere, and got drunk on what we'd done. Occasionally we had a small triumph."

"You don't sound very enthusiastic."

I had no answer to that.

"What was Berlin like?" she asked. "I read about the Paris riots in '68, but nothing about Berlin."

"Rougher than Paris. The police were much harder on us. The student radicals we met there had a saying that you were no one if you had not been *eingebluted*."

"What does that mean?"

"It means that you were beaten so badly by the police that you needed hospital treatment. A rite of passage which proved you weren't a police informer. Not that you went to hospital."

"Why wouldn't you go?"

"That's how *they* got to identify you, officially, after they'd taught you a lesson. They'd beat you black and blue and bloodied — *eingebluted* — then let you go so that no one could say it was them. They'd drop you near a hospital and wait to catch you as you walked through the doors. Foreigners were deported for riotous behaviour. Germans went to jail."

"Oh..." There was a moment's silence. She asked, "Did you really expect to change the world?"

I nodded.

A woman came out of a gaggle of people at the bar and walked up to us. She put her hand on the table, leaning over. "You coming to the next meeting?" she said to Woodie.

"Likely."

"Aye, right. It's at Margo's."

"I know."

"Got other things on your mind?" the woman said, looking over at me.

"Margo's," said Woodie, firmly. The woman walked off.

"Meeting?" I asked.

"To change the world," she replied. Was it irony in her voice, or grim determination, or something of both?

The pub was very noisy. People drank pints, round after round, and it had begun to show.

The food arrived, and we set to. Our booth was one of several that stood on a dais. The floor in front of us filled up with people talking, drinking and laughing. At the other end of the pub was a stage. Four long-haired musicians shambled onstage, and several people started cheering as instruments were plugged in. Once the band started playing I could hear very little else. The crowd swayed to and fro. Couples danced.

A man reached over and grabbed Woodie's arm to pull her

onto the dance floor. Before I could move she pushed him away, hard. He fell back with a laugh.

The crowd parted around two men fighting. One tore the other's shirt as he lurched at his opponent. Fists flew. "Outside! Outside!" everyone shouted, and the men were pushed from hand to hand to the door. One fighter had a bloody nose, but when they reappeared a few minutes later, arm in arm, there was no blood to be seen. His shirt front was missing, though, leaving the collar loose around his neck like a defrocked priest. It was impossible to hear a word over the noise. Woodie motioned me to finish eating. The fish was delicious. I was happy.

When the band took a break almost everyone went outside for a smoke, leaving us to enjoy the fresh air that blew in.

"Do you still believe the world is set up wrong?" Woodie asked.

"Yes, but Paris taught me that it'll take time to change that. A lot more time than I thought it would."

Woodie smiled. "Don't I know it," she said.

I went on, "We ran rings round the establishment, and it still won the election that was called to try to stop the riots and marches. I was so naive, so sodding naive. Losing the election was my wake-up call. I could see that the whole thing was too amorphous, and the timeline was too damn long. I couldn't wait forever. I had to go back to doing something that pays the bills."

"Pays the bills?" Woodie echoed. "Did you have to put that first?"

"For a while, yes. I owe my mother that. She worked bloody hard so I could get to medical school. I want to pay her back some of the money she put in."

"What's she do? What's her job?"

"She *was* a night clerk at the Hilton in Marble Arch. Now she's living her dream."

Woodie asked, "What's that?"

I felt strange saying it. "She's singing. She's with the Disney on Ice troupe that's touring South Africa." I smiled. "She's the voice of one of the princesses. She sings in the background while Mickey and Pluto skate around."

"Living a dream — how strange." She sat back and smiled.

"Yes, isn't it? People never guess. Now it's your turn. Tell me about you."

"Okay. Let's settle up and go."

"Go where?"

"Go round the trawler, like I promised. You still want to, don't you?"

Did she need to ask? I felt as if it must be obvious I wanted to go wherever she was going.

10

WE DROVE IN silence to the docks, between us an air of familiarity.

At the dock gate she got out and spoke to the night watch. When she returned she said, "We'll leave the car on the corner, so it's not so obvious. We're not supposed to go onto the dock... no tourists allowed."

We went through the side gate the man unlocked for us. He was very old. Woodie touched his cheek as we went through, and he smiled. "That's one beer I owe you," she told him. "Not more. Mary would kill me if I got you drunk."

"Get on with you, lass. Just don't fall in. There's more chance of that than of me getting drunk," he replied.

Water slapped against the dockside as we walked, the dark only occasionally relieved by lamps on the walls of buildings to the right of us. In the distance the hill behind the port loomed, hiding the stars. Then the clouds passed, and the cool bright light of a full moon lit everything so that I could see the way more clearly. Woodie walked purposefully in front of me.

At the end of the dock was a lone trawler, rocking gently with the swell. A gangplank led onto its deck, above my head. As she led me up wooden slats I had to hold the rope railings, but she didn't bother.

"Never been on one of these, have you?" she said as I stepped onto the deck's firmer footing.

"No."

"There's one thing I want to show you. Follow me."

We walked down a narrow corridor. As we passed the bridge I saw wide panoramic glass windows held in place by sturdy wooden frames. The wheel was smaller than I had imagined, its spokes larger. We reached an open cabin that had six flat shelves, as wide as a man, jutting from its walls. Cupboards under the ledges and at the sides of the cabin all had brass catches.

"Lie down on this," she said, tapping an upper ledge. The gentle rocking of the boat helped me on it. Woodie hoisted herself onto the one facing mine, and we lay down. It was very uncomfortable, and I said so.

"Right," she said. "These shelves are bunks for the crew. They're not even curved to stop a man falling out. The bleddy owners don't care how the men feel. I do this from time to time, to remind myself of what it must have been like for the men before."

"Before what?" I asked.

She did not answer. There was a silence. The moon went behind a cloud. We lay in the dark.

"A crewman has to provide his own mattress and bedding," she said suddenly, "as well as working for bugger-all in wages. The captain earns twenty-five times what they do for a trip, and the owner twenty-five times what a captain does. It's a wonder the men don't have to find their own food for the six weeks they're out."

"You hate that, don't you?" I said. "Injustice."

"Yes. You do, too." Was she telling me so I would know that she knew, or reminding me so I wouldn't forget?

She lay quiet. The stillness was disturbed only by the sound of wood creaking, and once or twice I heard the groan of rubber tires as they were squeezed against the dock by the ship.

"You like me, don't you?" she said.

"Yes. You know I do."

"I've been watching you. The patients like you, the nurses like you. You've a gentle touch, and I know you're honest. You're decent."

I did not know what to say.

She gave a soft sigh. I held my breath.

"I like you, too," she said, reaching across to me. I took her hand and kissed her palm.

"Oh," she said, "I knew you'd get it right." Then: "Not here. We'll go to my house." There was a catch in her voice.

We drove in silence, away from the dock, through quiet streets. She lived at the top end of one of the streets of row houses.

"We've to park my car off the ginnel," she said. "I've a spot there."

"What's a ginnel?"

She grinned. "Never heard that expression, have you?"

"Is it anything to do with middenrammers?"

"Only when they go down it."

We stopped at the end of a narrow laneway behind her house. It was sloped from both sides to the centre, down which ran a long, shallow drain.

"The ginnel," she said.

We went in by the back door. I found myself in a kitchenette at the end of a long single room with a large window that faced the street. The front door led straight in — no hallway. Two armchairs, standing on a bare linoleum floor, faced a fireplace. There was a smell of smoke. A full coal scuttle stood to one side, steel tongs buried in the coal.

"Let's go up to the bedroom," Woodie said. I looked round, but could see no stairs.

"I know," she said, "it's a puzzle, isn't it?"

She opened a cupboard door. Inside it was a narrow circular metal staircase. She climbed up it, and I followed. It was a tight fit.

I stood at the top of the stairs. There was a single bed.

"I changed the bed after Joe died," Woodie said pulling me into the room.

THE FIRST TIME we made love I said, "It's a long time since I've done this." It didn't last long.

She said, "It's been longer for me, I'll bet. I've not been with anyone for four years past."

We made love until I could no more. We slept and woke in bright Sunday sunlight.

I lay close to her and asked, "Why did you take me to the boat?"

"They're part of me, those bunks."

"Joe slept on those?"

"Yes. Even when they made him a captain . . . even then he slept with his crew."

"He made captain?"

"Aye, the last times he sailed out. He was the only good seaman they could trust who'd risk it. The only one they could cajole into doing a Christmas run." She sighed and said, "He came back from the first one, before the holiday, but not from the second, in the New Year. He and his crew were lost. In January, in the North Sea. That's what happens."

"Why did you say cajole?"

"No one in his right mind goes trawler fishing in the dead of winter. The bleddy rigging and superstructure get iced up, and if you can't get it off double quick, the ship turns over. You die in a couple of minutes in the water."

"Then why did he go out?"

She turned so that her back was right up against me.

"There were two reasons," she said, so quietly that I could hardly hear.

"They wouldn't give him any work because he was pegged as a troublemaker, always trying to get better conditions for the trawlermen and their families. He couldn't get hired most of that last year... until Christmas. That was one reason. And the other was we needed the money. I'd had a miscarriage and couldn't work. We were really short. If it hadn't been for me mam, I don't know how we'd have managed."

I felt her shiver. I pulled her hard to me, and the covers tight over us. I thought we slept again, for a short time.

WE WERE CLOSE from the get-go, and after the first time making love we grew closer. With her it was intimacy in every way, right from the start. Being with her felt like coming home.

When I awoke she said, "What's that poking into my back?" and breakfast was delayed again. Afterward I lay and looked around. There was a small ledge in the ceiling, about two-thirds of the way along. I followed it down one wall and, going back, down the other.

"What's it for?" I asked, pointing.

Woodie sat up. "These houses were built by ship owners for trawlermen. There were going to be two rooms up here, with a wall built where the ledge is. You know, to give families some privacy, kids from parents, old from young. Common decency."

She got out of bed. I could see she was angry again. She said, "Someone decided it wasn't worth spending the money to put in the wall. Privacy? What did they care? Owners know trawlermen are barely a step up from cattle and worth a damn site less." She banged the ledge. "One of them left out the wall, and the other owners followed on. Would have cost an extra five pound."

She pulled on some clothes. "Breakfast?" she asked.

"I need a pee."

"The privy's outside back. Or you can go out the front door, turn left and you'll see the communal one. You'll have a choice of eight stalls. One of them will mebbe be free."

As she climbed down the stairs she said, "Indoor plumbing was too pricey for the bastard ship owners to put in." From the bottom of the cupboard her voice came up. "The council's taken over the houses. Slowly, but surely, indoor plumbing will come. So will Christmas."

"I'll go in the garden," I said.

"It's why we bought this house and not one nearer my mum's. So we could always be sure of getting a seat when we most needed it."

11

WHILE SHE COOKED BREAKFAST I took stock. Lying against one wall was a framed front page of a newspaper, the *Daily Sketch*.

"What's this?" I asked.

"I keep meaning to hang that. If you look you'll see there's a picture of Lily Bilocca. You remember her, don't you?"

"You'd think it would be hard to forget a big lass like her, but I…"

"She started things going, led a bunch of fishermen's wives to Westminster. She spoke to Harold Wilson, eye to eye, about changing the way trawlers were fitted out to make things safer for our men. And she got it done. Or I should say *we* got things done, once she'd shown us the way."

"You were one of the women? But weren't they over in Hull."

"Look in the crowd behind Lily in that picture. You'll see me there. When I heard what she'd started me and a few others from

Sweport went to Hull. One of the best times of my life, right after the worst. I'd lost Joe three years before."

Bacon sizzled in the pan. "The girls I went with were like me; we'd all lost men to the sea. We couldn't abide it any more that our men were dying because the bleddy owners wouldn't rig out ships properly." She pulled two plates from the rack and handed them to me to put on the table. "Now at least they've got radios, so we know where they are, and they know what the weather's doing. They'll all be getting proper de-icing equipment, too... mebbe... A few ships have already, but that costs real money so..." She shrugged.

We ate bacon and eggs. She said, "Lily's not been able to get a job since. They've blacked her, the bastards. She keeps fighting, but she needs help."

"Was that what the woman last night was talking about when she asked if you'd remembered the meeting?"

"Yes. We stick together. We've had a taste of what women can do."

"You're still trying to change the owners."

"And the rest."

"The rest?"

It was Sunday. Bells were ringing, corralling the faithful and the timid.

Woodie heard them, too. She nodded her head at the sound and said, "We have to stop the Coopers and their like, and their Church, from hobbling us. If they get their way there'll be no abortions, no French letters, no Dutch caps, and for sure no Pill. Then there'll be no women's rights — because that follows as the night the day. If you're always pregnant you can't think straight, and your man has to work at whatever job he can get... Unless you've got money like Mrs. Cooper and can buy your freedom. Her dad was wealthy, from owning. She brought a tidy sum to that marriage, I'm told."

She made up the fire while I washed the dishes. There was an Ascot hot water heater, one of those small ones that sits above the sink with the gas pilot light at eye level. Hot water comes out instantly from its chrome pipe, but in a thin stream. You have to know what you're doing to make the most of it.

Woodie put paper on the grate, then kindling, then finally lumps of coal heaved onto the metal grate from the coal scuttle. Once the flame had taken she held a whole spread of newspaper in front of the fireplace to get a good draw going up the chimney. We sat on the couch in front of the roaring fire. When one thing started to lead to another she jumped up and drew the curtains.

LATER WE SAT and told each other our secrets till the fire waned.

"Let's go to the flicks," she said. "We can walk. It's not far."

We marched along at a good clip. It was early evening, not as cold as I expected. As we passed by the back of a dilapidated building she said, "This used to be a synagogue, but the Jews got frozen out, and now..." She gestured to an alleyway along the side of the building. "It's called Sin-a-go-go." On the ground, in the half-light, several used rubber condoms lay like spent white worms.

A woman appeared, walking with a limp. She had large breasts and hips, and dyed yellow hair.

"Hello, Edna," said Woodie. "What're you doing here, as if I didn't know?"

"Mind your own beeswax." Edna's brown eyes were not quite aligned properly. Her crooked smile was amplified by bright red lipstick. It was not well-applied. Neither was her mascara.

"You used to say that to me at school."

Edna grinned. "You were a bloody nosey prefect, always taking yourself so seriously, except that time we got you drunk at the football match. Then you weren't so high and mighty."

"I wasn't then, and I'm not now."

"Oh pull the other leg, it's got bells on. You're Queen of the May every day, or you'll know why."

Woodie grinned, nodded and pointed to the condoms. "You'll have to go to Leeds or Hull to get those from now on. I hear the Church elders stopped Jimmy's barber's shop selling them." She turned to me to explain. "That was the only place you could get them."

"There's more than one way to skin a cat," Edna said, waving two fingers at us as she walked away.

Woodie said, "She's a prossie. I'm not sure who her pimp is now, but that's her patch."

"You know everybody," I said, my arm through hers as we loped along.

"I've lived here most of my life, and it's not that big a place, at least not if you're talking about the fisher folk. I know her because her dad died alongside Jim that winter. We were close for a few months, what with the grieving and everything that went with it."

We walked in silence. Her stride was as long as mine.

"You can't get Johnnies in Sweport?" I asked eventually.

"Not any more. Contraception's against the Pope's rules, and the Church runs everything."

"How did Edna become a prostitute?"

"No money, no job, the wrong men in her life would sum it up. That and booze."

We were last in the queue for the pictures. It was a popular movie.

"I'd like a baked potato," Woodie said, pointing to a van that stood on the road halfway down the line.

"What'll you have on it?" I asked.

"Cream cheese and chives," she said. I chose butter and bacon bits. The potatoes, wrapped in silver foil, were cut in half to allow the fixings to mix with the hot centre. We shared. I liked her choice better than mine.

By the time we got inside the cinema there were no two seats together, and we had to sit on either side of an aisle. I saw Woodie say something to the man sitting next to her. He laughed, stood up and came over to me.

"You've got my seat, and I've got yours," he said. "You're lucky I'm here on my tod."

I asked Woodie what she'd said.

She grinned. "I told him I'd rather have your hand on my knee than his."

We spent the night together. In the early light she drove me to the hospital.

"I'll see you later," she said, and kissed me.

A FEW DAYS LATER I was third on call and taking the opportunity to catch an afternoon nap. My beeper woke me. Half asleep, I picked up the phone. George's voice shouted, "Flying squad! You're on! Come to the car park, now!"

I sat in the back of the old Daimler ambulance with Tripti and Our Joanie the midwife while George drove like a madman across town. Our Joanie steadied the grey and pale-green machine known as a Lucy Baldwin.

I loved Lucy, and so did most women in labour; it provided them with an anaesthetic mixture of nitrous oxide and oxygen. On paper the doctors and nurses could control the concentration of laughing gas a patient inhaled, but the real controller was gravity. A woman would hold Lucy's black rubber mask to her face and breathe in and out. After a short while her labour pains would lessen in severity. The system had a built-in safety valve: about the same time the pain relief appeared, the patient became semi-conscious and would let the mask fall. Minutes later the cycle would begin again. Lucy Baldwin had four large pivoting wheels that allowed her to be rolled easily in any direction. This made her a useful piece of equipment in the labour room and on Flying Squad emergencies. Gasmen were hard to find in Sweport, as elsewhere, and hospital O.R. work took precedence over trips into the unknown.

After a while I recognized the well-tended flower-bed area I had driven through with Woodie. The houses still looked neat and tidy. Once or twice I saw the reflection of our ambulance in windows as we raced past. Lace curtains waved a little with the draught.

"What are we going to find at the end of this joyride?" I asked as we swerved around another corner, our bell ringing loudly enough to wake the dead.

Tripti said, "We got a desperate message from a GP who made a house call on a young girl. He found her well-on in labour, which was a nasty surprise to him and, would you believe, her parents. It turns out that not only is she a primip, but that she is also a primip *breech*, who's got to delivery without any antenatal care, and with no one knowing."

"Oh Jesus, Mary, and Joseph," said Our Joanie. "What a mess!"

Tripti stroked his moustache, a frown on his face. He pushed his gold bracelet firmly up his arm, under the sleeve of his white coat. His greens fit him well. He was wearing O.R. clogs which, unlike mine, were hardly scuffed. He looked more like a soldier about to go on parade than a doctor on his way to an emergency. He slid open the window between us and the driving cab and said firmly, "George! Don't run through any more red lights!"

He turned to us. "He loves to do that, but it's not necessary. He doesn't understand that the problem with a breech extraction is that the cervix doesn't dilate well. The baby's bum isn't as good as its head for providing the necessary pressure, that extra oomph..." He leaned back. "We can afford a little extra time here to let maximal dilatation occur... if it's going to. Anyway, it is not my wish for Sunita to be a widow just yet."

Our Joanie gave me a look. Her look said she knew all about the problems of breech delivery.

As we turned down the street from where the call had come George rang the bell long and loud. A man's bald head appeared in a doorway. When he saw us he shouted, "Thank God you've arrived!" He was fat and sweaty. His waistcoat was unbuttoned, and his shirtsleeves flapped as he waved his arms. "This lass is in trouble. My God! What a shock I got when I found she was a breech! She's been trying to push, and its damn hard work to stop her. I'm sure the cervix is not fully dilated yet."

The patient lay on a couch in the living room of a small three up, two down. Her mother sat on the floor by her while her father stood in the hall, a grim look on his face.

Tripti said, "We've got to get her up on a table. Front room or kitchen?"

"Not the front room!" the mother hissed.

Tripti took a look in the kitchen. He came out and said, "Cover the table with a plastic cloth. If you've got something soft for her to lie on, put it underneath it. C'mon! Move, please!"

Our Joanie and the mother slid two sheets under the girl. She was silent, except during contractions when she cried, moaned, and looked exactly like what she was — a very frightened child.

We lifted her off the couch... "One, two, three!"... using the sheets, and deposited her on the kitchen table. Her legs hung over the end while sweat ran off her belly and onto the floor. There was the smell of meconium, acrid and familiar. All of us put on paper masks.

"Oh Mam!" The girl grabbed her mother's hand as another contraction came on.

"You and your husband take one leg each," Tripti said to the mother. "Put her feet on your hips." Then, "You'd better look the other way."

"You won't need me now, will you?" said the GP from the doorway.

"No." Tripti waved his dismissal. "Nurse, wheel in Lucy Baldwin."

"I'll do that," said George. "I've got to put the ramp in place first."

"What's your name?" Our Joanie asked the girl.

"Freda."

"How old are you?"

"Fifteen."

"Someone's in trouble," said Our Joanie.

"Too bleddy right," said Freda's father. "When I get my hands on him..."

"Not now!" Freda's mother said sharply.

George appeared, pushing Lucy Baldwin. Behind him the GP's car's starter could be heard, whirring very slowly. The engine coughed and then fell silent.

"Not his day," George said with a grin. "That battery's not doing too well; I may have to give him a boost." The starter whirred again, and an engine coughed into life.

"No!" said George. We heard the squeal of tires. "Couldn't wait to get away, could he?"

"Give her Lucy's mask," said Tripti. He pulled up a chair and sat at the end of the table between the girl's legs. He said loudly, "Freda, if the pains are bad, just breathe in and out of that mask, and they'll get less."

I heard Freda say, "Oooh! It's rubber. It smells weird! I don't want it!" at the same time as Tripti said, "The bottom is crowning." Then, "There's still a lip of cervix."

"Oh Jesus!" Freda shouted.

"Shut it!" said her mother fiercely.

"Will you need forceps for the head?" I asked in the silence.

"No. Watch," said Tripti.

I watched as he slipped a finger up and alongside the baby's protruding bottom and into Freda's vagina

"I can push the lip up..."

"Oh Jesus!" said Freda again.

"Stop that!" said her mother.

The baby was facing its mother's back, so its spine was uppermost in the air. I saw part of a squashed scrotum poking out below. It was red, crinkly and swollen. Tripti pulled at something, his wrist curving upward with effort. The top of a baby's thighs appeared. Tripti pulled again, but gently this time, and the rest of the leg, bent across the baby's stomach, came into view. As it slid out it was so pliable that it looked as if it were made of rubber.

"One!" said Tripti. He repeated the manoeuvre on the other side. This time the leg appeared with far less effort. Both legs and half of the baby's body hung down below the table top.

"Two!" said Tripti. "Nearly there, Freda."

"It's a boy," said her mother, a catch in her voice.

Freda gave a long sob. "Is he all right?"

Tripti took a small, green towel from Our Joanie and draped it around the body, slippery with meconium. Using the towel to keep a firm grip he pulled downward until the baby was left hanging, its head inside its young mother's vagina, its back toward us. The lower jaw was just visible at the top of an oh-so-thin neck, which seemed nowhere near strong enough to support any weight at all. The cord ran up into the vagina.

"Now for the clever part," Tripti said. "Let's give the cervix a chance to dilate fully." We waited for what seemed an eternity. I wondered if the cord was being compressed.

Tripti stood up, put his left index finger into the baby's mouth from below and took its feet in his right hand. With a swift, sweeping movement he lifted the tiny limbs up, over and between the inverted V made by the girl's legs. He used his left hand to guide the baby's head out of the vagina. There was a soft sucking sound as it crowned. Tripti looked like a magician pulling a rabbit out of a hat as he shouted, "Done and dusted!"

Freda tried to sit up.

"No!" said Our Joanie. "I'll give him to you in a moment. Hang on, love."

"That's the Mauriceau-Smellie-Veit manoeuvre," Tripti said loudly. "No need for forceps. Obviated most cleverly."

Later, after the cord had been cut, and the baby had cried, he laid it on its back on the kitchen counter. He bent its knees backward and then opened its legs slowly, leaning forward a little as he did so.

"Hips don't click," he said. "Good. I didn't dislocate them." He put his finger in the baby's mouth. "Good sucking," he said. He put his Littmann on the baby's chest. "Normal heart sounds," he announced a moment later. "Very healthy child, I believe. Wrap him up, Nurse."

We loaded Freda and her baby into the ambulance.

"You follow behind," George said to the parents.

It was a tight fit, so Tripti sat with George in the front cab. Our Joanie held the girl's hand. I sat opposite. Freda fell into an exhausted sleep.

"What a terrible shock for her parents," I said.

"Serves 'em right," said Our Joanie. "They didn't do their job properly. I know 'em. Never go to church. Never took their children there. What did they expect? Wait till Corrigan gets her hands on her."

I FOUND WOODIE IN THE autoclave room outside the O.R., setting out instruments for routine operative procedures: forceps, Caesars, episiotomies, and general suturing. She had to consult a list of what each gynaecologist favoured, because no two surgeons use the same set of instruments. She wrapped the sets in green cloth and then sealed the package with masking tape on which she wrote, in thick indelible ink, what was inside and who it was for. There were several packs in the autoclave and several more waiting to be sterilized.

"I was gobsmacked that a kid of her age could *get* pregnant, *be* pregnant, and her parents not know about it until she goes into full-blown labour," I said. "What the hell did they think her fat belly was from?"

"They didn't think. They didn't look at her."

"And the only thing Our Joanie could say was that it served them right for not being good churchgoers."

"Welcome to Sweport." Woodie opened the door of the autoclave. A blast of heat shimmered in the air. She put on a pair of oven gloves and took out several packages, replacing them with ones she had just prepared. As she stored the sterilized sets in a glass-fronted cupboard she said, "Won't be the last time you'll be gobsmacked in Sweport."

To one side of the cupboard an odd-looking instrument hung on a peg. It had the long handles of a pair of garden shears, but instead of the steel blades it had what looked like a baby's mouth. The upper jaw slotted into the lower one, giving it a prognathic look. The metal gums, which gleamed in the light, had been sharpened. "What's that?" I asked, pointing at it.

Woodie shivered and said, "It's a pair of Richardson's."

"What are they used for?"

"I don't want to talk about it."

"What?"

"Look 'em up in the library," she said. Then, "We going out Saturday?"

"Of course."

"My mam will have supper for us." She shot me a look.

"Good," I said. "It's about time we met."

I wondered what Woodie's mother was like. By this time I had seen pictures of her in the house and heard a few stories about her.

I WAS FIRST-ON for the next two days, and I was busy. Finally the rush was over, and I took a break in the common room in one of the beaten-up armchairs, my feet on the coffee table. My pager woke me. I called in. "You're on, lover," Woodie said into my ear, "they're cooking."

As I reached the Delivery Suite I heard someone screaming, "I ain't going up on that table! No! No! No!" This was followed by a scrabbling sound.

Someone shouted, "Alicia, don't be silly! You'll be ..."

Her voice was cut off in mid-sentence. Then she yelled, "Ouch! You little cow!"

I went to see what was going on.

A midwife, nursing her hand, leaned against the delivery table. A very pregnant young girl crouched in a corner, hair matted with sweat, face red and tears in her eyes. She wore nothing but a green overall, open at the back, stained with meconium and blood.

"She bit me," said the midwife.

"Go get it seen to," I said.

"Right. You're welcome to her." She left the suite.

I turned to the girl. "What's your name?" I asked.

"You ain't gonna hurt me?" she sobbed.

"No," I said.

"You won't let them hurt me, will you?"

"No. Of course not. It's Alicia, isn't it?"

Before answering the girl jumped up, ran round the table, barging me out of the way, and ran down the stairs. I chased after her, stumbling in my hurry. It took me a moment to get my balance. I saw her run into Ward One, the doors flapping closed behind her.

When I pushed them open I found her in the middle of the ward, thirty women staring at her. Some were shocked, others smiled, and one laughed. Alicia, now the centre of attention, grinned and bobbed her head. I walked forward. Before I could get near she turned and bent over to expose her backside and vagina to me. In a loud voice she said, "I'll let you bum fuck me if you promise that you won't let them hurt me."

I stood stock still, my face turning red. I did not know what to do. I wished the earth would open and swallow me up. Someone said, "Oh my God!"

Woodie appeared, carrying a blanket. She pushed past me and threw it around Alicia. "Stop messing about, my girl," she said. "You come along now. I'll set you right. No pain, I promise." She turned to me and said, "She's nobbut a baby, this one."

Some baby, I thought.

THAT NIGHT I spoke to my mother. The international operator took an age to connect with her counterpart in South Africa. That was 6,000 miles from Yorkshire; it took a while to make that sort of connection in 1970. Finally I heard my mother's voice: "Bry... What's it like there?"

"Weird, Mum. Not like anywhere else. It's all so harsh, like a scene from the Middle Ages. There are no soft edges."

"That doesn't sound much fun."

"But the good thing is that I've met someone."

A silence.

Then she said, "So have I, Bry. I didn't expect to, but I have."

I laughed. I was pleased for her. "Me neither, Mum."

"I might stay longer, Bry. Will you be okay if I do?"

"Sure, but I don't think I'll be staying on here. I don't know that I could."

"What about the girl?"

"She's not a girl. She's older than me. Her husband died at sea."

Clicking and several voices in the background — then my mother, back on the line: "Does she have children?"

"No."

"That's okay, then."

"What about your..." More clicking, and I heard several voices at once.

"I'll write, Bry," said my mother over the noise. "I'll write and send pictures."

I MET WOODIE'S MAM, Barbara, on Saturday night. Her house was two streets over from Woodie's. We walked there, arm in arm. I was happy. As we reached her front door there was a fluttering of wings. In the gathering dark I made out the ghostly outline of a bird. It flew over our heads and disappeared under the roof. A moment later another followed.

"Pigeons," said Woodie. "Dad used to keep them, and Mam's not got the heart to get rid of them."

Barbara was a small, stocky woman with a practical bent and a no-nonsense manner. She had small eyes, a gravelly voice, and lines down the sides of her mouth. Like her daughter she had been widowed by the sea. We sat in the single downstairs room around a wooden table. Its top was pitted and scarred. I ran a finger along one of the scars.

Barbara said, "That's what scissors do to wood when you cut along a pattern. I used to do dressmaking in my spare time when

I worked in the fish sheds. But I gave it up when I got my new job. No time."

"What do you do now?" I asked.

"I'm a receptionist for Dr. Van Kampen."

"He's a GP. His practice is close by," Woodie said.

"It's full-time work and then some. No more dressmaking." Barbara tipped her head, her face serious.

"He and Dr. Leander are close," Woodie said. "Dr. Van doesn't follow the party line, so most other doctors in Sweport don't like him."

"Helena is fond of Dr. Van, and he likes her," Barbara offered flatly. That was what she saw, that was what she said.

"Helena?" I interrupted.

Woodie gave me a look, and I shut up. Her mother said, "That's not what you call her, is it? She never liked that name, though I don't know why not."

"Leave it, Mam," said Woodie. She stood up. "I'll get the fire going. It's that miserable out; I'm still half frozen."

Barbara lifted a lid on a pot, looked inside, put the lid back on the tilt to let steam out. She opened the oven door, slid out the roast, and stuck a fork in it.

"Twenty minutes before dinner's ready," she said. "Let's sit and talk the while. You can shell peas if you will, Brian."

In short order the conversation turned to questions about me: how I got to Sweport, what my family was like ("Just you and your mother, then"), and where we lived ("London... well, you'll get over it," with a grin, which had Woodie saying, "Mam!"). Finally, when she was satisfied, Barbara said, "Okay. The roast'll be done. I'll take it out and let it set. You do the veggies, Helena, and then we can eat."

A short while later she said, "Open the beer, Brian, please, since you brought it. You'll find glasses in that cupboard. I don't like drinking from the bottle." I could see where Woodie got her managerial streak.

I relaxed as we ate. I asked Barbara how she had come to make the shift from gutting fish to being a doctor's receptionist. She was straightforward in her answer.

"When my husband died I took the insurance money and paid off the mortgage. Then I sat down for three months and did nothing. I knew one thing for sure: I wanted to get as far away from gutting fish as I could. Not because of the work, but because I couldn't abide watching the men going out to sea from the sheds."

Woodie said, "It was an awful time."

Barbara tilted her head. "Then I went to secretarial college, the oldest one in my class, I may say, and not the worst by a long chalk, either, and the rest followed."

"Never thought of moving away?"

"No. Sweport's where I was born, and this house has been my home since we married. That comes to mean something. And, even if I had the urge to leave, it went by the board when I heard of Dr. Van Kampen's job. I jumped at it."

"Why were you so keen to work for him?"

"Because of what he does to stop girls from getting in the family way."

"What do you mean?" I asked. "What does he do?"

Barbara put down her fork. "He fits them with the Dutch cap or the Copper T IUD." She added firmly, "And just this last year he's started prescribing those new oral contraceptives. Mind, they have to go to Hull or Leeds to fill the prescription, because no one around here will."

I stopped myself from saying that they weren't so new any more — that women in London and New York and Berlin had been taking the pill for almost a decade. And in Sydney, and in Toronto — all over.

She carved more thick slices off the roast, so different from Dr. Cooper's offerings. We helped ourselves to veggies again. We ate. There was a comfortable silence. I saw myself in the glass of the well-used sideboard with family pictures along its top, the centrepiece a fine photo of Barbara and a tall man standing by the harbour wall, arm in arm. I felt at home.

"He's the only one, then?"

"Yes," said Barbara, "more's the pity."

"There'd be less girls in the family way when they don't want to be if he weren't," Woodie said.

Barbara spoke firmly. "Those lasses who don't have a doctor like Dr. Van all get to sing the same song: there's never enough money, they're worn out from having babies, they hardly know where to turn, and they hate getting old before their time."

A door slammed in a nearby house, and I heard the sound of a car grind into life.

She said, again, "We — my husband Albert and I — thought, nay, we *knew* that's not right."

Woodie added, "There's something else. Dad admired Dr. Van because he makes no secret of the fact that he'll help a woman get an abortion. It takes some courage to do that around here."

"I don't want to talk about that side of things," said Barbara, her face flushing.

"Well, whatever, you can't deny he helps them," said her daughter. She paused and added, "I should say he *helped* them. It's all over now, Leander being so sick. There's no one to take his place. It's a crying shame!"

She stood up and stoked the fire, wielding the poker so hard that the fire grate clattered. I heard the sound of wings beating and scraping against something hard. It was loud and came from above our heads, near the chimney breast. It went on for a good two minutes, a wild, disturbing noise.

"You've upset the birds," said Barbara.

"Sod 'em," said Woodie. "It's time to get rid of them, Mam. You can't raise your voice or turn the telly up without them doing their pieces."

The clatter died down.

"Thank God!" said Woodie. "Between them and the bleddy Church there's no freedom around here."

Barbara started to speak, but Woodie interrupted her. "Don't argue, Mam! Don't bleddy argue! What the Church wants, the Church gets." The fire burst into life, colouring her face red.

Barbara stood up to clear the table, her features set, her head bent. She moved quickly. With a dish in her hand she said flatly, "You've always got something to say, Daughter."

As suddenly as it had come on, Woodie's anger dissipated. She gave a laugh and said, "Too right, Mam! I'll get you and me a soapbox each! Yours'll have to be bigger than everyone else's cos you're a little 'un."

I had heard about Woodie's temper from Arjun and had gleaned from the other midwives that it came and went in a flash. The trick was to keep out of her way when she exploded; she had a sharp mind and a sharper tongue. Nevertheless she was popular. We had talked about that once already, and she had said, "They like me because I'm fair and I make 'em laugh... at themselves, at each other and at me."

Barbara folded her apron, "Albert always told me it was harder to know if Sweport women were more trapped by their men or their religion."

Woodie said, "Whatever, Mam. The problem is that getting an abortion has become a thing of the past for Sweport. The Church rules. There's only Dr. Van, who'll write a referral to a gynae."

"So what's going to happen if a woman needs one?" I asked.

"If they've enough money, girls in trouble go to Paris — would you believe? — to keep it secret from prying eyes. If they don't have the wherewithal, and around here most of them don't, they have the baby and then go to hell. That's where most of them end up. Only it's called the bingo hall or the pub."

I could see the resemblance to the tall man in the picture. She said, "The biggest pity is, if they're desperate enough, they go to back-street abortionists, what Dr. Van calls the gin-and-coat-hanger Johnnies. Then they're really in trouble. Hell would be better."

"Don't be dramatic," said Barbara. "It doesn't help. We've got our work cut out, and it'll take time, a lot of it, so we mustn't run out of steam too soon."

I said, "I did GP locums while waiting for an Obs job to come up. I've worked all over, town and country, and never come across anywhere as raw as Sweport. It's like that bloody fish-gut smell, one-off and no escaping it. There's no give-and-take."

Barbara said, "That's East Yorkshire for you." She sounded proud of it.

"I want a smoke, Mam. Leave the dishes till we come back in."

"Aye. If you have to."

Woodie and I went outside. The night air was sharp, and my throat burned with each drag. Behind us I could see Barbara washing the dishes.

"She's so stubborn," said her daughter.

When we came back in Barbara said, "Brian, I hear you've had to deal with two cases the past few days of girls not old enough to be out of school, pregnant and frightened to death. Two in one week, in a place as small as Sweport." She shook her head.

"The secret primip breech was a real eye-opener," I said. "She was just plain lucky. If she'd not been handled properly she and her baby could have died. Tripti was a lifesaver." I shook my head and added, "House calls are an education."

Barbara nodded. "Dr. Van says that seeing patients at home is how he measures the difference between the fiction patients tell him and the truth."

Woodie grinned at me as she said, "That other girl, the one on the ward who offered you the special bribe — she shocked you, didn't she?"

"You can say that again. What's with her?"

"She's a halfwit, been on the game for a while. Mind, she's only just fifteen now."

"What happened, exactly?" said Barbara. "You never went into details."

"It was Alicia, you know the one who lives with her dad over on Rebuck Street. She was in labour and frightened to death, so she offered Brian something special if he would take her pains away."

I held up my hand. "Don't go any further; I'll be embarrassed all over again."

Barbara said, "Her dad's a bad lot, a drunk like *his* father before him. He's the one likely putting her round to get booze money, though he must know it'll kill him sooner or later. The pity of it is that it killed his wife first. And she didn't drink."

15

"*DON'T FORGET* the meeting is at Doreen's," Barbara said, as Woodie and I got up to leave. "We set it so you wouldn't be working that day."

Walking back to Woodie's house I asked, "I take it your mam is part of that women's group?"

"Yes. She's been in it from the beginning."

"Why did she look embarrassed when you talked about abortions?"

"It goes against her grain," said Woodie. "Dad was the one who persuaded her that it was okay to be involved. He was a mechanic who worked on trawlers all his life. For him it was cut and dried, like repairing a broken engine. If a girl was in trouble, and an abortion was what she needed, then it was okay to help her. He and my mam were brought up good Catholics, and it took a lot for her to come round to his way of thinking. It still costs her. I know she's glad that no one will be coming to Dr. Van for that any more, though she won't say so."

"It is hard to change from what you've taken to heart," I said. "But sometimes you have to. You get boxed in by life."

"Yes."

After we'd walked on for bit she asked, "Did you like being a GP? When you did locums?"

It took me a moment to reply. A man walked past us, weaving a little, up to the front door of a house. He banged on the door, shouting, "Martha! Let me in! I've left the bastard keys somewhere!" The door was flung open and a whiff of warm air and beer engulfed us as the man brushed past the woman.

"Yes. It was fun."

"Not boring? All sniffles and sore throats?"

"You can't ignore the simple stuff. It's a key you need to have turned to be able to help people when serious problems turn up. I liked it, because I soon learned that you never know what's coming through the door. Never. I like having to stay on my toes."

"Good thing," said Woodie.

"It'll keep me young," I said.

"Or kill you."

We reached the ginnel. A solitary light shone far down as we turned toward her house.

I said, "Helping people works well for me. It's just that I think I'll enjoy doing Obs and Gobs more. There's no rush like delivering a baby."

"No, lover. There isn't."

Though it had not been raining, everything around us glistened. The wind blowing in from the North Sea had decorated the streets with spray. I shivered.

"Not used to Sweport yet?" Woodie said.

"It's warmer by the hospital. It's that little bit farther inland."

"I didn't mean that. You said that everything was raw here. Is it as bad as it was when you first arrived?"

"No, but that's because of you. It was no picnic for us in London, but there wasn't the same edge to everything. I get the feeling there's not much hope in this place."

"That's the truth," she said. She cleared her throat and said, "You don't talk much about your mam and how it was."

"I had it easy. All I had to do was get good marks. She had worked to support the three of us: me, my gran and her. And found the cash to take the occasional singing lesson. But it all paid off."

"What about your dad? You never talk much about him."

"He died in the war, like I said. If the truth be told I was a Lend-Lease baby."

"What does that mean?"

"My father was a US serviceman sent to England with thousands of others to fight Hitler, along with tons of equipment. Gran always said that the men were the best part of that Lend-Lease program. On one of his furloughs, the story goes, he met my mum. They were together a very short while before he was sent to Europe and got killed. They were engaged, but..."

She broke the silence that followed with: "They never married?"

"No. Anyway, who cares now?"

"Not me, lover, not me, if you don't." After another silence she took my arm and asked, "Do you ever think about what he was like?"

"Not any more. I used to. I used to imagine how he died. It was always because he was doing something heroic, that kind of thing." I found it difficult to go on.

She said, "My dad used to say there were things I did, habits I had that were exactly like his mother's. I never knew her. She died when I was just a baby, so I don't know exactly what he meant. But he said it often enough, so it must be true. Perhaps you'll see things in your kids that can't be traced back to anyone, and they'll be a clue to what your dad was like."

My head felt full. I felt a blush rushing up my neck. I said, "They'll have to be different from things I see in you and your mother, then, and what you tell me about your father."

She stopped dead still. I turned to face her.

"That's the most roundabout proposal of marriage I ever heard," she said.

"You know I love you," I said.

There was a silence, which she broke by saying, "And I love you."

"Is that a 'yes'? Will you marry me?"

There was a much longer silence and then she said, "Yes."

We kissed, and everything was different because I was suddenly part of a pair. Gran used to say that man is a two-backed animal, only she said it in Russian, which sounds more dramatic than English.

Woodie said, "There's so much to decide. I don't want to be in a hurry to do anything now. I need to get used to the idea."

We reached her home and went in by the back gate. As we walked past the privy I said, "Wouldn't you like to stay at my digs for once?"

"No," said Woodie, "it's against regulations. If it weren't, Arjun would have a queue of nurses outside his door every Friday night he wasn't on call."

I grinned. "You know he's working through the nurses alphabetically? He started with a girl whose name began with A and went onto a girl whose name began with B, and so on."

Woodie grinned back. "They've twigged what he's up to, mind. He's got a surprise coming."

"What kind of a surprise?"

But she would not say. Nor would she come to the prefab.

"Not yet," she said.

"I feel as if we're doing something wrong, but we're not.

It's hard to relax properly if no one's been told."

"Let's get away for a couple of days," she said. "Somewhere no one knows us."

As we went inside I said, "How about London? We could stay in a hotel for a couple of nights — and I could show you the London I know, just as you've shown me Sweport"

"Yes," she said. "That's a lovely idea."

16

TWO WEEKS LATER, on a Thursday, we were on the early train to London. As soon as it left the station I felt free. We went to the restaurant carriage to have breakfast.

It came with spiked orange juice, as I had ordered, and the heady mixture of freedom and booze obliterated our self-restraint. In no time we were laughing and fooling with each other. An older woman on the other side of the aisle did not know what to do. She clucked, loudly, which made us more juvenile in our behaviour. I loved it.

I was nuzzling Woodie's neck when I felt her stiffen. I looked up to see Mrs. Cooper walking past, with two other women. They were all dressed to the nines, in elegant coats and expensive shoes. One of them was slim and the other was fat, with dyed red hair and powder caked on her puffy pink face.

Mrs. Cooper stopped, looked us over and said, "Good morning, Dr. Davis. Good morning Sister Woods."

As soon as they had passed, Woodie put her arm around my neck and, pulling me closer, replied in a toffee-nosed accent, "Oh hello, Mrs. Cooper. Bleddy good day, isn't it?"

As the trio went through to the next carriage we burst into laughter.

"God!" I said. "They must have heard that."

"I hope they did. They run the Church's anti-abortion committee. 'Bake sales for babies' is their best slogan. But it works. That Mrs. Cooper's one tough bitch, and she's in charge. The slim one was Mrs. Staples, who sent you the bottle of whisky — remember? You delivered her grandson. The fat powdered one was Mrs. Durnforth. She's as bad tempered as can be and full of herself. Mind you, she got her comeuppance last year."

"How so?"

"The fishermen can't work in winter, so they go on the dole. She wangled herself a job handing the envelopes out at the Ministry office, so she could play the grand lady. One day she said something about being lazy to Stewart Briggs. He has the shortest fuse in Sweport, and when she passed her remark he leaned over and smacked her face. He's a big fellow. Broke her jaw. Cost him three months in jail, but that didn't bother him. Free meals, he said. She quit. We all fed his wife and kids. It was worth it."

"Tough place, Sweport," I said.

Woodie grinned. She said, "The one to watch is Trudy Cooper. She can get the troops out, and no mistake."

St. Pancras station appeared, and a few minutes later we were getting off the train. We did not see Mrs. Cooper or her two companions, not along the steam-shrouded platform, nor in the queue for taxis. Though it was raining outside it was warmer and more inviting than Sweport. I was happy to be home.

We spent a great two days together going round London by way of my memories. I had to tell Woodie everything that made each place special. Hugging each other tightly we marched round my haunts, lock-stepped by love.

We changed hotels the first day. We stayed in one just long enough to make love on the huge, soft, king-sized bed. Neither of us had slept in one before. Then we checked out. We did it just to see the receptionist's face when she realized how we had used her upscale hotel.

"Do I look good enough to be a prossie?" asked Woodie, as we walked down the hotel steps to the cab that we had ordered.

"Better. Love those shoes."

On Saturday we took the train back to Sweport.

"We won't be a secret any more," I said.

"We weren't before," said Woodie, "except from Mrs. Cooper and her kind — and they've never mattered where it counts."

17

IT TOOK ME A MOMENT to recognize the first patient I encountered in Ward One, on the Sunday after our London trip. She was lying in bed, propped up in a sitting position. There were two IV bags running into the vein on her left forearm, one piggybacking into the other.

A man sat by her bedside, crushing a cap in his hands — tall and heavily built, with the ruddy features of a seaman, and angry.

I looked at the name on the board hanging from the end of her bed. The woman was Clara Cawl, on whom I had performed my first solo forceps delivery months earlier. I went over to the Sister's desk and looked at the chart. One of the nurses, a middle-aged prim and proper, nodded her head and said, "She's landed here because she tried to get rid of a pregnancy the gin-and-coat-hanger way. It's terrible what she's done to herself, or mebbe it was one of the Romanies who helped her out."

"Romanies?" I said. "You have proof of that?"

The nurse blushed. "Well, not exactly. Mebbe it was not one of them. But someone helped her into this world of trouble. She couldn't have done it alone."

I leaned over to get the chart. "What's with her, then?"

The nurse stopped my hand, saying, "You've no need for that. I can tell you. She's likely got a perforated uterus, is running a fever and is as sick as they come. Who knows what is cooking inside her."

"God knows, that's who," another nurse said, then, "Dr. Chak's coming to take another look." She lowered her head and whispered, "Go and talk to her. You've treated her before, haven't you? Mebbe she'll tell you who made such an awful mess of her."

I went back to Clara Cawl. Her face was flushed and sweaty. There was an unnaturally bright look in her eye, and, incongruously, she was smiling vivaciously. Her hands fluttered everywhere. She was talking a hundred to a dozen, to anyone nearby, to her husband, rattling on about the shopping that needed doing, where to find the makings for the children's school lunches, what her husband's mother said yesterday, how hard it was to clean under the stove and would he move it next time he was ashore and, anyway, when was he due to sail out, she couldn't for the life of her remember.

Through this all her husband said not a word. His angry expression had faded to flat fear. He reached out and took Clara's hand. To my surprise, he put it to his cheek.

Still Clara kept talking, as if nothing untoward was happening. She did not even stop when her husband said, "Clara! Clara, don't!"

Tripti joined me. He said something to Clara's husband, who got up and walked away. We drew the curtains.

"She's diaphoretic, feverish, bordering on mania," said Tripti in a low voice. "She's a classic gram-negative septicaemia. The next twenty-four hours are critical."

He put his hand on Clara's stomach. She winced and stopped talking.

"There's guarding and tenderness, possibly worse than a couple of hours ago when she was admitted." Tripti said to me. He jerked his head toward Sister's office. Thank God that it was Corrigan's day off.

Once there he said, "I've examined her. Balloting that uterus during the vag exam got an extreme reaction. She almost jumped off the bed. But there's no bleeding from her vagina, so either there's no laceration and we're dealing with infection alone, or, more likely, it's closed up with clot for now, with trouble hiding in the wings. I'm running high-dose gentamicin and penicillin in those drips." He grimaced. "Let's hope she doesn't go deaf as a result. We won't get the blood cultures back for forty-eight hours, so we're working in the dark, though I'm fairly certain I know what they'll show."

A nurse came in. He turned and said, "There you are, Staff... About Mrs. Cawl... we'll have to open her up tomorrow if she's still got a high fever and is as sore as she is now. That's if the anaesthetists let us. They know I suspect gram-negative septicaemia, which means that, if things go badly, her kidneys could fail any time."

To me, he said, "They won't gas her if they think there's a serious risk of her dying on the table. It would screw up their mortality figures."

I was busy in the Delivery Suite until early evening. After a bite of supper I went back to the ward to see Mrs. Cawl. She had changed, and not for the better. She was so quiet and still, I thought she was asleep. Her face was pale grey, ashen. Small beads of sweat lay on her forehead, and her lips were dry. Woodie was by her bedside.

"How is she?" I asked.

"Not good. Look at that finger."

Mrs. Cawl's right hand lay on the covers. Its index finger, slightly curled, moved across the blanket as if tracing an invisible pattern. It ran backward, forward, round and round, ceaselessly. At times it moved quickly; occasionally it lay still, but never for long.

"That always means trouble," said Woodie.

"I thought she was sleeping," I said.

"No. She's semi-conscious at best."

"You're on night shift in Delivery, aren't you?"

"Yes. I have to get back there. I only just heard about her." She stood up.

"I'll come up with you," I said. "I'm on, too."

We climbed the stairs and were busy as soon as we entered the Delivery Suite. Much later, long after daybreak, I got a call from the ward.

"You'd best come down," said Staff. "It's Mrs. Cawl. Dr. Chak is here."

Woodie and I went down together. Tripti was by the bed, a frown on his face. Mrs. Cawl was Cheyne-Stoking, a pattern of respiration, once heard never forgotten, in which breaths have a particular rasp and are few and far between. "She could keep that up for hours," said Tripti, "but I don't think she will. Has anyone called the husband?"

"He phoned a few minutes ago. He's coming with the kids," said Staff. She turned to Woodie. "You know her," she said.

"Our husbands worked together for a few months. We got to be friends for a while, but it didn't last after Joe died."

Woodie sat down. "Her finger's stopped," she said. We waited. Clara sighed.

"It won't be long now," said Woodie. She took Clara's hand and stroked it.

Everyone on the ward waited, speaking in muted tones. The television was off. A quiet dread hung in the air. After a while, Clara Cawl stopped breathing.

"Crash cart!" Tripti shouted."Code Four! Call the anaesthetist!"

The crash cart, a spindly steel mobile trolley with three shelves that held adrenaline, lignocaine, oxygen cylinders, masks, intubators of all sizes, and a defibrillator, was only ten feet away. He need not have shouted, but you cannot be quiet when a young person dies despite your best efforts.

For a good twenty minutes we tried to resuscitate Mrs. Cawl, but she did not respond. Overwhelmed by bacterial attack her kidneys had failed, and her other organs had followed suit.

Later I spotted her husband in the quadrangle. He had seen his wife's body. He was standing stock still, his broad shoulders slumped forward. A car drew up, and an older woman stepped out with three children and a baby. Mr. Cawl burst into tears as they ran to him.

"Mam," he shouted, "she's gone!"

"Oh Jesus!" she said.

He stood, his arms down around his children, pulling them in tight. The old woman crossed herself. They were all crying.

18

WE WERE IN WOODIE'S HOUSE, sitting on the sofa. She fidgeted, rubbing its arms as she spoke, her words coming in short bursts.

"He was always saying how much he loved her. It used to grate when we went out to the pub together, him going on and on." She stood up and walked to the window that overlooked the street. "When it comes down to it he loved her to death," she said. "To death."

A little later she added, "He's so bloody religious. Clara told me he was against contraceptives — cos it's 'against the will of God.' He was always telling her that."

She opened the window, which was hard because the sash often stuck. It banged against the frame, finally. "He bleddy *knew*, that 'God will take care of us,' day in, day out. She tried to see it his way, but I could tell it didn't fit her."

A cold draft filled the room. "It was fine for him. He went out on the boats, leaving her with four children to worry about, with no money and precious little help. Then, to rub it in, she's not home a few months with number four, and there's a new one on the way. Of course she tried to get rid of it. Who can blame her? What the hell is he saying now, I wonder?"

"Close it," I said, pointing to the window. "It's bleddy cold. If you're so jumpy I'll get you something to calm your nerves. D'you want a whisky?"

"No. I'll make a tea. You stay put." She slammed the window down and went to the kitchenette at the back of the house.

There was a knock on the door. I got up and opened it. Two police officers were standing there, one man very much larger than the other.

"Is Sister Woods in?" the large one asked.

"I'm here," Woodie said loudly. "What's it you want?"

"Can we come in?"

THEY SAT OPPOSITE US, around the kitchen table. "This is a delicate matter," the spokesman said. His smaller companion looked around the room, taking no trouble to conceal his prying.

"Go on," Woodie said. "Spit it out."

"You knew Clara Cawl, the woman who died yesterday, didn't you."

"Yes. What about it?"

The big man leaned forward as he spoke, so that his face was much closer to Woodie's. "Where were you on Friday last?"

Woodie did not back away. "In London."

There was a pause. The thin man asked, "Can anyone confirm that?"

"I can," I said.

"And you are?"

"Brian Davis. I'm her fiancée. We went to London together on Friday morning. Why do you need to know where we were that day?"

"From our enquiries we've learned that Mrs. Cawl went out that afternoon in good health, leaving her husband with the kiddies. When she came back, two hours later, she was clearly unwell. She was much worse on Saturday morning, so he took her to hospital."

The big policeman said, "Where you visited her."

Woodie said, "We both did. Yes."

There was a silence.

"You're a doctor, aren't you?" the thin one asked me.

"Yes."

"You two are... engaged, you said."

Woodie and I answered together. "Yes."

"Is there anyone else who can vouch for where you *both* were on Friday?"

"What the hell do you mean?" Woodie said angrily. "What are you getting at?"

The big man stood up. "Someone performed an illegal operation on Mrs. Cawl. You both have the expertise to do it. So we need to know where you were when it was done."

I felt hot. Sweat broke out under my armpits.

Woodie was fuming. "I've just told you."

"And I've confirmed it," I said.

"And you two are to be married. Which means you're close. Very close."

"I have the hotel bills," I said.

There was a silence.

"Sit down, please," I said to the big man. He did not move.

"One of you could go to London, check in to hotels while the other was still in Sweport. In theory, anyway," the smaller officer said.

"What the bleddy hell are you saying?" Woodie was shouting now. "That I did an abortion on Clara? Or that Dr. Davis did? That we *conspired* to do it, and covered our tracks?"

"Don't raise your voice," the bigger one said. "We're simply asking the question. That's our job."

"I'll bleddy give you..." Woodie shouted, getting to her feet.

I could see the fit was upon her, and who knew where that would lead, so I jumped between them, facing him and with my back to her. I said, as calmly as I could, "We took the early morning train to London, the Express. There's another fast one at night, from St. Pancras, getting in at ten. The only other train back to Sweport is the slow one, which leaves London at three o'clock, getting in at eight. We were seen on the morning Express by Mrs. Cooper, Mrs. Durnforth, and Mrs. Staples. You'll know those ladies, well-known for their work on the anti-abortion committee. You'll believe what they say, I am sure. We couldn't have had anything to do with what happened to Clara."

The big policeman sat down and took out his notebook.

"Give me their names again, please," he said.

"Mrs. Staples, Mrs. Cooper, and Mrs. Durnforth. They're bound to remember."

After they had left Woodie and I sat together on the sofa. I put my arm around her, but she shook it off. "Don't," she said. "You shouldn't have stopped me. I'd have given them a piece of my mind and then some."

"I could see that," I said. "But it would only have given them an excuse to be more in your face."

"Who the hell cares!" She was becoming angry again.

"It's my experience that the police go after low-hanging fruit," I said. "The question is: Who made the police think we were that."

MUCH LATER, in bed, she said, "I'll ask Harry Hurst. He's a good guy, even though he's a rozzer. I've known him forever."

"What will you ask him?"

"Who put the word in about me and Clara Cawl. And what those three old cows say about us being on the train when they're asked."

I lay thinking, against a background of sounds of the port: grunts of a trawler making its way, waves slapping against the dockside, someone shouting, "G'bye!," the trundle of a bicycle over cobbles, and other muted-for-the-night sounds of life.

Woodie, who had to work the next day, slept. I did not. I knew we could not rely on people behaving well; we had to ensure that they did. As chance would have it I was off call, which was a good thing because I had much to do.

In the morning I drove to Mrs. Cooper's house. The old Ford Pop looked incongruous next to the expensive car parked in the drive as I walked to the front door. There was no answer when I rang the bell, so I walked round the back, through an ornamental gate with bars of different-sized bamboo struts. There I found her, in a Japanese-style garden, dressed in old clothes, with a floppy hat covering her eyes: the patrician at work.

"I know why you've come," she said, bending to deadhead a flower.

"You do?"

"The police called." The secateurs in her hand made a soft grating sound as she worked.

"Then you told them you saw us that day, on the train."

"I certainly saw you, but I can't remember which day. We go to London quite often... for meetings." She straightened up and looked right at me.

I knew then that we had a fight on our hands, so I said, "One of the Ten Commandments says you must not tell lies."

She flushed momentarily, then put the secateurs into the pocket of her apron and said, "That impertinence will cost you dearly." In a dead-calm voice she continued, "Get out. Get out, now!"

At the gate I turned, "Tell your travelling companions that we have another witness."

"Then you won't need us, will you? Why did you bother to come at all?" For the first time she smiled.

I sat in the car with the engine running, wondering if the receptionist from our two-hour hotel visit would remember us, whether management was honest enough to keep a record of our short, delinquent stay, or would simply pocket the cash with which I had paid.

I found Mrs. Staples through the phone book. I recognized her as soon as she opened the door. She was not surprised to see me.

"Mrs. Cooper called you," I said.

"Yes." She did not invite me in.

"What will you tell the police?"

She stood, looking at me. Then she closed the door.

I did not find the third woman, not at home or at the nursery school she owned. Clearly word had got out. I got back to Woodie's after nightfall.

IT TOOK TWO DAYS to get an answer during which time I found it difficult not to dwell on what had happened. For once I was glad that work was so demanding.

Woodie called me. "We're okay . . . just." she said.

"What do you mean by 'just'?"

"Meet me in the café, and I'll explain. At one of the outside tables."

The sun was shining, and there was no wind. She had a coffee ready for me. "Thanks," I said, kissing her. Sparrows pecked at crumbs by our feet. In London they would have been accompanied by pigeons. Here seagulls, voracious and unforgiving, took their place.

"Harry says Mrs. Staples confirmed seeing you on the Express. Bill, the big ox, wouldn't say who told him we'd been to see Clara."

"What about Mrs. Cooper and Mrs. Durnforth? Did they back her up?"

"His exact words were, 'It's good to have friends like Mrs. Staples.'"

"That means the other two didn't confirm seeing us."

"What do you think?"

"Jesus."

She smiled and said, bitterly, "*He's* not here, whatever people think. This is Sweport."

19

A SMALL INDIAN WOMAN, not more than 4 feet 9 inches, sat on the side of the bed in the lying-in room, her feet barely sticking out of the green hospital gown. She was relaxed, which was a surprise because when asked she said this was her first child. Most primips are nervous. In their shoes, going to deliver a child for the first time, I would be, too.

"How far along are you?" I asked. "How often are the contractions coming?"

"Every few minutes," she said.

"Do they hurt?"

She nodded, but without much conviction.

"Well, I'll get a nurse and examine you," I said. "Every few minutes means we have time in hand." I had not noticed any contractions while we had been talking. I had not put my hands on her swollen belly or clerked her.

"Please don't go," she said. "It won't be long."

"Don't worry," I said. "I'm just going into the hallway."

"Please don't go," she repeated. She lay down on the narrow bed, pushing the pillow to one side, so she was lying flat.

I smiled to reassure her, repeated what I'd said and turned to call for a nurse.

"Doctor!" Her voice sounded more urgent. She made a kind of clucking sound and then said, more quietly, "Doctor..."

I turned back, and, to my astonishment, I saw the baby's head between her spread legs.

That evening I told Woodie, "She didn't make a fuss at all. I had no idea that she was fully."

"Most of the time we're not really needed," she replied. "Most of the time Nature gets the job done without us."

"Yes, perhaps... But what was so odd was that she made no sound at all."

"Not odd — different."

"You know what they say," I said.

"What?"

"A doctor gets the patient he deserves," I said with a grin, and she laughed.

We did that a lot because we were happy. She liked to laugh, and I did, too.

She said, "When I was training, my teacher was a nun who had spent time in Africa, most of it in Kenya. The stories she told were hair-raising. One of them was about the time she visited a small hospital in the bush outside Nairobi. She said the place was desperately short of equipment and staff. There was one fridge with two packs of blood hanging there that looked weeks old. What made it worse was that in the distance she could see the Aga Khan's hospital, which was made of shining white marble and was beautiful, spotlessly clean, and really well-equipped. Anyway, my teacher said she was shown the children's ward, which was attached to a small Obs unit. I remember her saying, 'I thought the unit was empty because there was no sound coming from it.' I couldn't see in from where I was standing, next to a baby's crib. But when I was taken inside there were three women in full-blown labour, on hospital beds, which had only bedsprings for them to lie on. They made no sound at all. In Kenya, childbirth is a silent process, even if you're lying on rusty metal."

"Not like here," I said. "The midwives make as much noise as that. Sometimes more."

20

IT WAS MY TURN to take the Contraceptive Clinic, which had been set up by Dr. Leander. Every second week in a corridor outside a disused ward, on two rows of chairs that faced each other, a clutch of women sat with stockings rolled down around their ankles, waiting to be shown how to use the diaphragm or to be fitted with the Copper T IUD. They looked a little lost — almost the way that refugees look, I thought.

A nurse got the women ready for the fitting; that day, Woodie was there to run the clinic. Each patient was ushered into a makeshift cubicle and asked to put on a gown after taking off her skirt and underpants. I would then come in to do a vaginal exam and put in trial caps until satisfied with the fit. I would give the cap back to them to hold, to bend and twist, so they became familiarized with it.

"How do I get it inside me?" was the inevitable question.

"You stretch the cap on this inserter," I would say, holding up the plastic device that looked like a chicken's drumstick shorn of its muscle, slightly curved, with notches at either end on which to stretch the cap. "You put it inside your vagina with the bend facing down toward your backbone. If you do that, when you slip the cap off the inserter it will lie in front of the cervix, making a solid barrier."

"What happens if I drop it?"

"Wash it and start again. Watch out, though. It's rubber. It may bounce."

One woman said to me, "It looks like a Hula Hoop with the insides filled in."

It did not take long to size a woman, using one of several caps provided by the company that made and sold them. The woman would practice stretching a real cap on the inserter, then I would leave her alone to insert it. Woodie and I would return a few minutes later and examine her to ensure it was lying in the correct place. About one in five managed to put it in incorrectly — but, as I said to Woodie, by the time they left everyone was good at inserting their own Dutch cap.

"Needs must when the Devil drives," was her reply.

Toward the end of this particular morning I got a surprise when I entered the cubicle. Sitting on the side of the bed with her gown undone to show her breasts, fat belly and pubic hair was Edna. She looked like a carved fertility goddess from South America.

"Hello," I said.

"Hello, yourself." She stared at me with an unblinking gaze.

"Come to get fitted, have you?"

"That's right. Come to make sure there'll be no problems, no unwanted kiddies. I think using a cap as well as a Johnnie is like wearing a belt and braces to hold your trousers up. But you wouldn't know about that, would you? That's only for fat guys or very thin ones, and I can see you're neither of those." She smiled again, in a practiced way.

I went through my routine, examined and sized her vagina and then left her alone to insert the cap I had chosen.

I was waiting next to Woodie when four people walked into the ward. One was Mr. Cooper, another was Sister Corrigan. The third person, a tall, thin man with greying fair hair, had a bony nose and a predatory manner. It took me a moment to recognize the fourth person. Finally it clicked. He was the onion man from the train, last seen months ago.

"Hello, Mr. Berk," Woodie said to the tall, thin man. "What brings our Hospital Administrator to this neck of the woods? And who is the gentleman?"

"Mr. Kelsey is the head of the hospital's executive committee, Sister," said Mr. Berk. "We are here to..."

But he was interrupted by a loud, "Fuckin' hell!" and then again, "Fuckin' bloody hell!" coming from the cubicle behind us.

We all froze as a Dutch cap, greased and gleaming, rolled out from under the curtains. It wobbled across the floor, taking a circuitous route before coming to rest on the polished toe of Mr. Berk's black shoe.

Curtains were flung back, and Edna appeared, her body, naked, except for the hospital gown across her shoulders, plain for all to see.

A sharp breath broke the shocked silence.

"I dropped the fucking thing," she said. Then, seeing our stares, she raised her voice and shouted, "What are you all looking at. Ain't you seen any of this before?"

With great aplomb she walked over, picked up the Dutch cap and pointed it at the onion man. Winking lewdly she said, "I know *you* have, you old skinflint! I've seen you around."

With a scream that shook the window panes, Sister Corrigan burst through the group and ran at Edna. Reaching her, she delivered a resounding slap to each of the girl's cheeks, shouting, "You hussy! Get yourself away! I know what you are, you disgrace — you whore! You're not wed, and you've no right to be here!" Then she hit Edna hard in the chest, shouting, "Get out, out!"

Edna staggered backward, flung her hands up and pushed Sister Corrigan away. She turned, grabbed her clothes and ran out of the ward, the hospital gown flying behind her.

The ensuing silence was broken only by the clack of Corrigan's heels as she walked back.

Mr. Cooper said to the onion man, "Now you know why this clinic should be closed. It cannot be good for the hospital's reputation..."

Woodie shoved past Cooper to put her face close to Corrigan's. "Who the hell gave you the right to hit a patient? Who gave you the right to throw a patient out of my clinic? What has being married to do with being fitted with a cap, anyway? Who do you think you are, you dried up old cow?"

I saw the hair rising on the back of Woodie's neck. Fearing she would do something irrevocable, I got between her and the target of her anger, just as I had done when she confronted the two policemen. "You've no right to discharge one of my patients without my permission, Sister Corrigan," I said. "You'll be lucky if she doesn't sue you for assault."

The remaining patients stood up and shuffled away, their stockings still around their ankles, refugees leaving a war zone.

The onion man gave a laugh. "She'll do nothing of the sort. I'm a magistrate — I've seen her in court. That lass has been fined for prostitution, by me and others." He touched his pencil mustache and added, "She knows to keep her place. If she dared to lay a complaint like that I'd make damn sure it was thrown into the midden, where it belongs."

I said as clearly as I could, "That would make you a midden-rammer, not a magistrate. If the cap fits..."

Woodie grabbed my elbow.

Quick as a flash the onion man said, "Fancy yourself as Saint George, do you? That tart a maiden in distress, and me the dragon?" His face reddened as he hissed, "You're nothing, just a young southerner with a big mouth who has no idea what's what in the real world. You mind what you say, or you'll end your life as a middenrammer and be glad of the work."

Cooper stepped forward, saying, "I'll take care of this—"

But before he could say anything else Corrigan shouted, "Bounce that commie boyo out the door, like you bounced the quare one before him, Mr. Cooper! Bounce him, bounce him! Who needs their kind here!"

Cooper hesitated, and I felt Woodie pull hard at my arm. "This clinic's over. We're leaving. You clean up the mess you've made, Corrigan," she said in a loud voice.

She jerked my arm again, pulling me away. It took all my self-control to keep silent.

Cooper stretched his hand out behind him, across Corrigan's chest. "Enough!" he commanded. As we reached the door I heard him say, "This space could be much better used, Mr. Berk. The surgeons at the Infirmary are always on the lookout for overflow beds. If they used it, your net income from the Ministry would get a boost."

Mr. Berk looked around, found a box of latex gloves, put one on each hand and, with dainty gestures, cleaned his toecap. "Your suggestion is very well-worth following," he said, straightening up. "There will be no more of these clinics until the Board makes a final decision next month." He peeled off the gloves off and threw them in a bin, its lid clanging shut in emphasis.

Woodie and I walked down the hospital corridor. I said, "The quare one?"

"The SHO before you was queer and didn't hide it. They made his life very difficult, and in the end he quit."

That night we lay in bed, talking.

"Did you see Berk's ears?" she said. "They're hairy. I hate that." She rolled up against me, so that we were spooning. "I know why you jumped in," she said. "I was close to losing it."

I held her tight.

"Thanks," she said. With a little laugh she said, "That's why I did the same for you, my Saint George." She turned over to face me.

"Let's see your lance, then," she said.

Toward dawn I woke. I knew instinctively that she was awake.

"What's on your mind?" I asked.

"I can't stay at the Maternity any longer," she said. "They'll have it in for me for certain now. They'll make up something to discredit me or get me reprimanded, mebbé disbarred. God knows what I'd do for a living, then."

My heart sank. "Where will you go?" I asked. I could not visualize a world in which she was not close to me every day.

Sitting up, she said, "I'm going to apply for a job as a District Nurse, here in Sweport. That way you and I won't be separated, at least for now, and I'll still be in touch with what's going on."

We would still be together. I had to take a moment before saying, "This is a huge change for you. Are you sure it'll be okay?"

"Yes... no... But I'm going to give it a try."

I leaned over and kissed her. "You're brave," I said.

She smiled at the idea. "No I'm not; I'm practical. If it doesn't work I'll find something else."

A foghorn sounded, and a shutter banged against a window frame. The year was drawing to a close. She added, "But I'll be doing what I've always wanted to do."

"How do you mean?"

"I'll be visiting people in their homes, checking to see if they're coping after coming out of hospital, meeting their families, dressing wounds, that kind of thing. I'll be helping where it really counts, which is the main idea."

She got out of bed and went downstairs. I heard her get the fire going. It was a cold morning. In few moments the smell of burning coal wafted into the bedroom. A little later she brought breakfast upstairs.

Back in bed, with toast crumbs around her mouth, she said, "What's more, it'll give me a chance to help girls in trouble."

"Is there a job?" I asked, stroking her back. I loved the curve of her spine.

"Yes. We were talking about it at our last meeting. There's little that goes begging around us. Nurse Briggs retired last month. I'm going to apply."

"You sure you'll get it?"

"I'd bet money I'll get a good reference from Cooper and Tripti, and even old hairy ears. They'll be glad to see the back of me because I'm too independent for their liking. They want another witch like Corrigan, brainwashed and nasty."

"*I'll* give you a reference," I said.

"As what?" she asked, lying down.

21

MY HOLIDAY WAS COMING UP, two weeks in which I could do whatever I wanted. Woodie was just settling into her new job, and I did not want to leave her side, so I was faced with a problem as to how to pass the time until she said, "Dr. Van wants to go away for a couple of weeks. He needs a locum, and they're hard to get around here. Sweport's no one's favourite destination." She took a breath and, after a pause, plunged in, "Would you do it? You'd earn money, which is always a good thing, and you'd get to know more about my town, my people."

My lover loved her people with the fierce devotion a mother has for a sick child.

"Have you talked to him about this?"

"I mentioned it."

"And what did he say?"

"That he'd like to meet you."

I had enjoyed all the GP locums I had done. One problem with working in hospitals is the ubiquitous internal politics, and that was certainly the case in Sweport. But I had come to terms with the problem because you cannot practice obstetrics without having hospital privileges.

As a solo general practitioner you answer to yourself. Politicking is not something you have to worry about. With all that had happened, the more I thought about it, the more appealing it became — the idea of taking a break and working on my own.

"What's he like?" I asked

"Different," she said. "He looks old-fashioned, but he's not."

She was right. I met Dr. Van at his place of work, an old house off the main road to the docks. His brass plate hung on the railings that surrounded a small grassy patch in front of the entrance door. There were sunflowers in his garden, up by the house. They brightened the place. It took me a little while to realize that they were plastic.

Dr. Van sat at a rolltop desk beside a large window with a blind that started halfway up it. There was a fireplace with iron firedogs, and a gas-fed fire with false wooden logs. He did not get up when I went in.

A man in a dark suit worn over a striped shirt with a stiff white collar, the doctor had greying tufts of hair, long spikey eyebrows, a large nose and deep creases in his face. After looking at me carefully he rose, very tall, and gave me a firm handshake. "Good day," he said, "I am pleased to meet you. I have heard only good things about you, but, then, the messenger is biased." I could detect traces of a Dutch accent. "I understand you and Helena are to be married," he said.

"Yes."

"*You* have not been wed before."

"No."

"She has. I told her that she would fulfill of one of Dr. Johnson's sayings. Do you know what that might be?" With a mischievous expression that changed his whole demeanour he said, "Remarriage is the triumph of hope over experience!" He let out a huge guffaw.

We talked shop for a bit. I must have satisfied his requirements because he ended our discussion by clapping me on the shoulder and saying, "Let's have a schnapps to seal the deal."

As we drank he said, "Helena has had bad luck in her life. First her father, then her husband, lost at sea — a scandal, they should never have been asked to go out at that time of the year. And just before that she'd had a miscarriage. You know about that, don't you?"

"Yes." Where was this going?

He said, "It was a blighted ovum. She was in the first trimester, thank goodness. One in six pregnancies, as you are aware, end that way. She was terribly upset — because Helena is one of those women for whom the child has meaning far beyond its gestational age. It has personality from the moment they know they are pregnant. After the miscarriage she was off work for three months. She had postpartum depression."

"I did *not* know that."

"I was at the hospital with her when the pregnancy came to an end. I should say with *them*. The whole family was there. She actually fainted while lying flat, because of shock. I got her husband to lift up the end of the bed while they ran around finding the wooden blocks." He added, "One day the Sweport group of hospitals will be able to afford modern hospital beds. We are still in the Middle Ages here, in more ways than one."

We talked some more: about how he'd come to Sweport, about Dr. Leander's sickness and what it meant, about the Second World War. He had served in North Africa.

"I learned two things from my war," he said. "One is that Rommel was a very good general, and the other was how to shave in tepid water, using a helmet resting on a tank's track as my sink. I don't know which was of more value."

I liked him. Woodie told me later that he felt the same about me. I was to start in two weeks.

22

WOODIE AND I SAT on a bench overlooking the harbour. It was a warm October day. Below us two men hefted a crate of beer into a powered rubber dinghy. One climbed in.

"You never told me you had postpartum depression," I said.

Woodie shivered. She said, "I don't like to think of it. Ever. But now you've brought it up, let's talk and then leave it be, for good."

"What was it like?" I asked.

She took a long moment before replying.

The man in the dinghy started the outboard motor and sat on a wooden cross seat. The other man climbed in and pushed off with a short oar. Neither man was wearing a life jacket. The dinghy headed out into the bay, threading its way past other, grander boats.

"It was like being inside a huge black box. I couldn't see my way out of it. I could sense the sky, and that there was a world outside the box, but there was no doorway, no window. I felt nothing for the longest time. Everything was black."

I took her hand in mine. She let it lie there.

"How long were you inside that box?"

"Forever." She shook her head. "In real time, about three months."

"What happened?"

"One day I got cross. Someone said a stupid thing. At least *I* thought it was stupid." She took her hand away and waved it in the air, in an angry gesture.

"What did he or she say?"

"He said that I had only had a miscarriage, and very early on at that. He said it was not like losing a real baby."

She stood up. "That was the worst of it, the realization that most people did not understand that a miscarriage was not *just a miss* for me. I had lost a child, my child. They thought, eight or nine weeks, that's nothing. Well it was not nothing to me. For those couple of months that child was everything."

She walked to the wall that ran along the harbourside. I joined her.

"His words made me angry. It felt as if someone had lit a fire inside me, and as it got hot, I got better. The box started to shrink. One day I was inside it. The next I could see over the top. Then I was bigger than the box. Sometime later, God I don't know how much later, it was as if I could hold the box in my hands and only when I looked inside did I become depressed."

"And now?"

"I've got you. The box is so small it fits inside my pocket, like one of a set of dice. I've stopped trying to open it."

What she said made me feel good.

In the bay one of the men took out a fishing rod. The other had his hand inside the beer crate. A seagull clacked, relaying news.

23

DR. VAN'S SECRETARY, Miss Fowler, had bright red cheeks and a sharp nose with a dewdrop hanging from it. She led me to the same back room in which I had met him. It must have been the back parlour, in the days when this was a private house. As we passed down the corridor I caught a glimpse of a waiting room full of people, likely the formal dining room back in the day. There was a trail of wet boot prints from the front door. It was raining.

I had learnt when doing locums that, afterward, I would be able to remember the first patient and then only one or two others, the remarkable ones. The rest would blend into each other because I met most people only once. This is one drawback of pinch-hitting in medicine, because people's idiosyncrasies are the salt that makes the bread-and-butter work interesting — occasionally, fascinating. "There's nowt so queer as folk," as they say in York-shire. The other drawback is that "Tincture of Time" is a large part of all cures. It invariably reveals the truth and is a valuable ally which it is not usually available when you are a sub. Its absence may cost the patient and the physician.

Miss Fowler said, "Ring the bell when you want a patient sent in."

"Thank you," I said with a smile, which she did not return.

I sat in the captain's chair, where her boss had sat when he interviewed me. It rocked back easily. I rolled from side to side on the wooden floor. I was the captain of my fate, and I loved the feeling. Above the rolltop desk's leather-bound blotting pad, cubbyholes were filled with different forms and ballpoint pens; an ornate inkwell that contained a paper clip but no ink stood to one side.

I took out my new Littmann stethoscope, pulled my jacket into shape and rang the small brass bell. This locum had begun.

The first patient was a big, blond woman, in her late twenties, who sat down without being asked. She knew the drill. Her khaki-coloured overall fitted only where it touched. It fell open, revealing two large pink knees and stocking tops. She wore rubber boots and smelled of fish; clearly she had come straight from work. She leaned forward and bared her left arm, on which was an angry-looking rash. Red weals and blobs embroidered flaking skin from wrist to elbow.

"Does it itch?" I asked.

I had no idea what the correct diagnosis was. Dermatology is a discipline that relies on having seen the problem before, coupled with a good memory. I had never seen a rash quite like this (and small differences mean a lot with skin problems), neither in real life nor in a text book. I felt incompetent, which reinforced my feeling that the only good thing about being a dermatologist was that there was not much emergency work.

"Course it does." She gave me a hard look and then pulled down her sleeve. "It's erysipelas," she said, firmly. "I get it from the fish scales that fly when I gut the sods. They're like flying sandpaper. This'll go if I take Amoxil, 500 milligrams, three times a day for ten days." She pointed at the script pad lying on the desk and said, "Give us the prescription, then."

"Right," I said with relief, and scribbled her instructions on the top sheet. I tore it off and handed it to her with a flourish.

She laughed as she left the room. Clear as day, I heard her say to someone in the waiting room, "It'll be your turn soon. You're in luck. His nurse is right to clang on cos he's good-looking."

Later that morning I made house calls in among the row houses fronting the harbour. I was staying in Woodie's house on Nelson Street. The other streets were Wellington, Prince Edward, Victoria, and Albert. Over my two weeks' locum I walked to calls in all those streets. They looked so much the same that the col-our of the front door was the only thing that distinguished one house from another. That was not true of what I found inside — there was a world of difference between neighbouring houses, depending on the personality of whoever was indoors. When I told Woodie how much fun I found that, she said, "You like people, Brian. It's a strength."

I developed a routine: up to the house, a sharp knock on the door, no waiting, a push, and once inside: "Shop! It's the doctor!"

Two calls stand out. When I plunged into the first house I found myself in a dank cave, heated only by a coal fire. The fur-niture was old and worn, the walls sparsely painted. There were no rugs on the wooden floor. Three women wrapped in shawls sat round the hearth.

"He's upstairs," said one.

They were drinking tea out of mugs. They did not offer me one. A radio was playing *Mrs. Dale's Diary*.

I walked to the back, opened the cupboard and climbed the circular metal staircase to the single room upstairs. Its walls were dripping because this bedroom was heated by a stove that issued water, heat, and paraffin reek in equal measures. The protruding lip that ran from wall to wall across the ceiling, and should have been a wall, stood out in the half-light from the stove. At one end of the room was a double bed. At the other end, only partly partitioned by a cupboard, were two single beds. One, under the solitary window, was small and empty. In the other, which was full-sized, lay an old man.

He coughed and waved at me weakly with the stump of an arm, cut off just above his wrist. Dr. Van had told me that many of the seamen had lost fingers, hands, or arms, severed by equipment that had broken loose during storms or amputated by steel hawsers whipping through the air. "The wind and weather rip them free and then they cut as well as any surgeon's knife," he said. "One of the men said it was as if he'd been hit sharply on the arm — it was a shock when he found his hand gone."

The old man did not have the strength to sit up. He could not stop coughing. Green phlegm and blood stained his single pillow. When I listened to his chest I heard bubbling everywhere. He had a low fever, his pulse was up, his blood pressure unmeasurable and his face grey. "How long have you been like this?"

"Week or two," he said in a weak voice.

"Who sleeps in the bed next to you?" I asked.

"Grandson..."

"And in the other bed?"

"Daughter and husband, when he's home off the boats." Even saying this exhausted him.

"You need to be in hospital," I said.

He shivered. "Mus' I?"

"Yes."

He shook his head. "No."

"YES," I said loudly. "You'll infect your grandson if you don't get away. And the others."

A tear appeared at the corner of his eye. "I'll die there," he said.

"No. You'll get better there."

"Pull the other leg, it's got bells on," he said. Then, "I'll infect the boy?"

"Yes. I hope you haven't already."

"With what?"

"Maybe TB"

He took a moment to digest this information.

"He's got no cough. Nor her."

"Good. Let's stop it happening, then."

He stayed quiet. "Okay," he said, finally. With great effort he sat up and reached over to his grandson's bed. He patted the sheet and said, proudly, "He's a good footballer." Turning, he said, "Let's be having you, then."

The ambulance men had a hard time getting him down the spiral staircase. They had to carry him between them, off a stretcher, one holding his shoulders, the other his legs. He looked like a set of sheets with a white face attached as they wrapped him round and round to the bottom.

"Wear masks," I'd said before they went upstairs. "I think he may have TB"

I was right. So was he, because he died a couple of weeks later. His family needed six months of treatment, PAS and INAH — those standbys that still worked, thank God. I'd seen what TB did to people, what state they were left in afterward, but I had never been so close to active tuberculosis outside a hospital, and I was shocked.

"It's a disease of poverty," I said to Woodie. "This is England in the 1970s, for pity's sake. We've the National Health! For all I know I'll find leprosy next."

"Come on. Look around you. This is Sweport, where people are treated worse than cattle. They're poor, nobody cares. It's what they deserve. Poor people get sicker more often than rich ones, because they're more stupid, we all know that. You shouldn't be surprised — that attitude is what we've got to change."

One night, late, a woman knocked on our door. She was very upset.

"We need a house call," she said. "I've no phone, please excuse me for coming round."

"S'no mind, Mrs.," said Woodie. "Come in. Can I get you something hot to drink? It's that cold out."

"Oh no! I can't stop, luv, but thanks for the offer. It's my son. He's been sick for three days. Please come, please hurry!"

I put on my overcoat and the flat cap Woodie had given me. "It'll make the folk feel you're almost one of them," she had said. "Almost."

As I picked up my bag, the woman said, "He's had a high temperature on and off, and today he's not talking. That's not like him. He's a chatty boy."

Her house was bright inside, and warm: a Bible was on the kitchen table, and candlesticks were on the mantel. The usual stairs — circular and difficult to manage in a bulky coat. I stuffed the hat in my pocket as I followed her up and around and around to the bedroom.

The child lay in a bed separated from his parents by a curtain hung from hooks in the ceiling. There was a small chamber pot under his bed.

"Let's have a look, then," I said, pulling back the sheets.

The boy lay quiet, his eyes closed, sweat on his forehead. He did not move his arms or legs and his chest heaved up and down rapidly. With each inspiration his ribs stuck out, only disappearing when he let his breath go. His cheeks were bright red. I motioned to his mother and she opened his pyjama jacket. There was a rash across the whole of his body. Red and pink, it lay in the yellow skin, rather than on it, looking like the outline of land that you see on a map of the coast. Red was land, yellow the waters between.

The child's forehead was boiling hot. He did not react when I touched him. I flicked his eyelashes. He did not flinch. I put my hand under his head and lifted it from the pillow. His neck did not bend. Its muscles stood proud, sharply defined. I lifted his head higher and his whole body rose up from the sheets as if made from a single piece of wood. He screamed. Shocked I lowered him and asked, "Has he been vaccinated against measles?"

"No," she said. "I... we... don't believe in vaccinating our children."

"He has measles meningitis," I said. "I'll call an ambulance."

"I'll go," she said, spinning down the stairs. "I know where there's a phone." I heard her say to someone, "God preserve him! Pray for him!"

WOODIE AND I TALKED over supper that evening, as couples do.

"Will the lad be all right?" she asked me.

"No. He'll be lucky to live. Epilepsy'll be the least of it. God! I thought everyone vaccinated their children."

We went to the pub to get out, walking arm in arm.

"Ayoop, flower," someone said to Woodie. "You look grand."

Woodie blushed and squeezed my hand. "Ta," she said. "You look grand tha'self."

We reached the pub. I could hear people shouting and laughing.

"Buy you a drink, Doc," said the barman, when we were inside. I saw people looking at us.

As we sipped our beer Woodie said, "You know what this means, don't you?" She stroked the side of my glass.

"What?" I asked.

"They've taken you on."

I did not know what to say.

24

FOR ONCE THE CALL to my mother went through quickly.

"I got your letter," she said. "You didn't send a picture."

"You'll see when you meet her." I lay on the bed in my prefab. Looking up I could trace cracks in the white pebble-dash ceiling. The phone's black handle lay on the pillow by my head.

"When are you getting married, then?"

"It's not decided. Things are a bit up in the air right now."

"Already?"

"No, not with Woodie. We're close. I mean at work — my boss has taken against me. I can't do anything right."

"Is that her real name?"

"No. That's what we all call her. It's Helena."

"That's better. What's her family like?"

"There's only her mam. Her dad was lost at sea, like her husband."

"Poor woman. What a terrible thing to happen."

Because I was cold, I had my surgical greens on under a white coat, but still the damp seeped through. As second-on-call I was required to be present on hospital grounds. By now most of my clothes were at Woodie's, so I had no sweater to hand. I pulled the bedcovers over me. I could hear rain beating against the metal roof.

"What did you do to get your boss riled?" My mother sounded apprehensive.

I told her what had happened at the Contraceptive Clinic.

"You're kidding. It rolled right up to them?"

"Yes. Onto his shoe."

"Your boss's shoe?"

"No, the Hospital Administrator's."

My mother laughed. "Well, it was an accident, wasn't it? Why did that turn your boss against you?"

I described the argument and what had been said.

"You've always been quick to stand up for the underdog," was her comment. I knew she had other things to say, but she held back.

"Is that a compliment?" I asked.

"Yes, Brian." She changed the subject. "How are you in yourself?"

"I'm very well."

"That's what comes of being in love. I should know."

"Who is it, Ma? Tell me about him."

When we finished talking I had a short nap and awoke in the dark. I turned on a light and reread the letter that had been sent to the staff living in the prefabs. Over Dr. Berk's cramped signature its single paragraph reminded us that no visitors were allowed to stay overnight in doctor's quarters without written permission and then only on a night-by-night basis.

Because second-on-call was a misnomer most days, I walked over to the hospital to get a head start on the work that was bound to be waiting. In the gloom the building's lights shone brightly.

Passing the doctor's common room I heard a shriek. I opened the door and stopped dead. Arjun was there with two nurses. He was on his hands and knees, with one of the nurses on his back while the other, who was really good-looking, was sprawled on an armchair facing them. She had a bottle of beer in her hand and was shouting, "Giddy-up, horsey, Giddy-up!"

"Jesus," I said.

"Join us!" shouted Arjun. "Come on, Brian! We need another mount! Nora has to wait her turn, otherwise!"

"Not bloody likely," I said. "You'll get fired if anyone catches you."

"Oh no," he said. The nurse's white apron had fallen in front of his face. In a muffled voice he said, "They're not staying overnight, so I don't need Berk's permission, do I?"

"Don't talk daft. You know what I mean. What about work? You're first-on."

"Not till midnight, you demi-Yorkshireman," he said, collapsing on the floor to more shrieks of laughter from the girls. "How is your better half, anyway? It's been ages since I've seen her."

"She's fine, thanks."

"That's good." He sidled over, sat between Nora's legs and said, "Trade with me, dear boy, please. I have my hands full right now, as you can see. I'll do your next first-on, I promise."

I agreed. As I left Nora was stroking his head.

ARJUN AND I met at around six a.m., in the Delivery Suite. He sat by the window, a cup of tea in his hand, a smile on his face.

I said, "What do you think of that letter from Berk?"

"Nothing."

"It's hardly nothing."

"It was directed at you, Brian. Who else? In case you and Woodie decided to make a day and a night of it."

"Rubbish. It was directed at you, of course."

"No, not at all."

"Come on. If they'd caught you last night..."

"Nothing would have happened."

"Why not?"

He leaned over, smiling. "I'm a wanted man, Brian, that's why."

"For Christ's sake, don't talk in riddles. It's too early in the morning."

"I'm not. They want me. I'm telling you the truth."

"Who?"

"I knew as soon as I arrived I was a desirable target." There was a pause. "The Church wants me, that's who."

"You're mad."

"No, anything but. See, I'm a doctor, I'm unmarried, and I chase nurses for a hobby. I can do no wrong. If I get a Church girl pregnant, I'll marry her — and to do that I'll have to convert."

"You're Brahmin! Why wouldn't *she* convert?"

"Get real. They hold all the cards. This is England, not India. They could stop me taking my next job — and other things, if they put their minds to it. And Nora must have told them that I don't care about religion, one is the same as another when it comes down to it... do this, don't do that, listen to the priests, that's the important part. They're all rubbish based on lunacy. When you see what's going on in the world, how can any rational person believe someone else knows the right answers?"

Jessie the midwife came in, and he stopped. When she'd gone he said, "Nora is the only one who's kept her distance. She's a cracker, isn't she? I've waited a long time to get to her, but I've done it. You've seen her; it'll be worth it."

"I think you imagine everything."

He stood up. "Your one fault, Brian, is that you're so blinkered you see only what's right in front of you. Let me tell you how it is." He tapped his stethoscope in his palm as he spoke. "You picked the wrong nurse, one they can't control, so they'll get shot of you like they did your predecessor, the queer. One thing's for sure: they'll never give you another job here. You and Woodie are troublemakers. They're betting that when they force you out of Sweport, she'll go, too. Two birds with one stone."

With a final flourish he said, "*My* bet is that they won't give you a good reference, either, so an Obs job will be hard to get, but you never know."

25

WOODIE AND I WERE in the garage at the top of the street. Her car had broken down again, and the garage owner, Bill, was trying to sell her a new one. "I'll bring it round for you to look at," he'd offered. As we waited, I told her about Arjun's latest escapade and what he had said.

She laughed about the horse racing. "That Nora knows which side her bread is buttered. She's played him, and he's taken the bait — hook, line, and sinker. Now she's reeling him in. She was smart not to sleep with him."

Bill drove up in a pale-green Ford Anglia.

"What do you think of the colour?" Woodie asked me.

"What's the difference? As long as it goes without any trouble."

Woodie said, "That's you all over. Arjun is right, lover. You're so focused that peripheral stuff slips by you."

Bill said, "This is a good runner, Woodie. I wouldn't sell you anything bad. Your old Popular's done for. The big ends have gone, and the gear box is a mess."

"What's *been* wrong with this one?" she asked.

He said, "The only thing we've had to do is weld a new piece of metal under the driver's seat, where the pedals were. It was rusted through, because the old lady never put in a water catcher. She hardly ever drove it, but when she did the water pooled there."

"It's okay now, is it?"

"I wouldn't steer you wrong. Not you. Why don't you try it for a couple of days?"

"I like the way that rear window goes in," she said, "and the colour."

"This car's the one for you, then. Look, luv, you try it out to be sure, and you know my price. I can't say fairer than that. You won't do better, I promise you."

We drove it home. It ran better than the Pop, was more comfortable, and had a heater that worked. All that did not stop me looking down at Woodie's feet as she braked, to make sure the road did not suddenly come into view.

"I know I can trust him because I delivered two of his kids," she said when she caught me at it. "And his mam's a friend. That's the upside of living in a small place."

"I'll buy it with you," I said when we got home. "We're going to split everything half and half when we're married, aren't we? So let's start now."

She sat down at the small kitchen table. "That's another first for me," she said. "You're not like the men around here. They like to keep control of the money."

"I never thought of it any other way," I said. "Did Joe keep control of the money?"

"No. I earned more than him most of the time. Anyway, he came round to my way of thinking very quickly. He was enlightened, you might say."

"It would be hard to be any other way with you."

"Cheeky sod! Come here, and I'll give you a black eye."

Later, I told her about my conversation with my mother. "It's weird talking to my own mother about both of us being in love with someone new."

"I'll bet it is." Woodie smiled. "Is she going to marry him, whoever he is?"

"It sounds like she will, though she didn't say so in so many words."

"She's not fully committed, then." Woodie smiled as she added, "Not like you, lover. Not like you."

Much later, she said, "Brian, I'm going to Leeds for three days: Friday, Saturday, home Sunday evening. It's a course for work. Mandatory."

"But I've got the weekend off!" I complained.

"Well, Friday you're working. Saturday there's football and wrestling on the tele to keep you busy. And Sunday you're invited out."

"What? Where to?"

"Dr. Leander wants to meet you, so Dr. Van said if you agree he'll take you over. It'll be worth it, I promise."

26

"*HE'LL BE IN HIS CONSERVATORY*," Dr. Van said as we drove, "preparing plants for his garden."

"I thought he'd had a stroke," I said.

"Yes. But you'll see that its first things first with Lee. Since his wife died the garden is his passion." He grated the gears as he added, "Time has made us a couple of old bachelors, against our will, I may say. My wife died two years ago."

"Have you a family? Someone nearby?"

"A daughter in Devon is as close as it gets."

We found Dr. Leander at the back of his house: a large man, wearing an apron over casual but expensive clothes. His shoes were highly polished. He had a huge head with only a little hair at the temples. Long bags under his eyes and sagging cheeks gave him a basset hound look.

"I wanted to meet you after I heard about the fracas at the

Contraceptive Clinic." He put down the trowel he held in his left hand. His right was firmly in the apron pocket.

We walked into the house proper. He rang a bell, and a woman appeared. "Tea, please, June, for three." He turned to check. "Unless you'd like something stronger?"

"Not yet," Dr. Van said.

The room we sat in was filled with paintings, rugs, and silver objects.

"Tell me about that fracas," Leander said as the tea arrived. Using his left hand he slipped his right forearm into his shirt front, so that it made a makeshift but effective splint.

I recounted the events as best I could.

"That awful woman," Leander said. "I couldn't get rid of her, hard as I tried. They stick together. The Church looks after its own." He got up and walked carefully over to a small side table. "Look at this," he said, gesturing to two piles of papers side by side. Both of them were headed *Terminations of Pregnancy*. "On the left are the original documents..."

"I've seen them before," I said, pointing at the right-hand pile.

"Oh, when?" Leander asked.

I told him about my dinner at Dr. Cooper's house.

"I loaded boxes of them into his car for him. He told me they were for the administration to keep a record of what happened in the Delivery Suite, week by week. He talked, I loaded. He wasn't pleased with me. Neither of them were, he nor his wife, Trudy."

"Why not?"

"I didn't agree to give their church group a talk about my time in Berlin and Paris."

Leander snorted. "She's not used to having people say no to her."

He opened a cigar box and offered me one, his left hand trembling a little.

"She will not accept that denying abortion saves babies, but kills mothers," he said.

The box was waved at me again.

"No thanks," I said, "I don't smoke."

"Good man," he flashed a smile. "One vice less... Well, even so, if you're asked, tell my nurse you're the one responsible for the smell of smoke, will you?"

I nodded, smiling.

The cigar lit, Leander said, "What I find hard to forgive is that the Coopers and their ilk think they can reconcile their behaviour with the wording of the Ten Commandments."

"What do you mean?" I was taken aback.

"The commandments state, *Thou shalt not kill, covet thy neighbour's wife, lie...* generally transgress. But they say that to each person alone; hence, the repeated use of the word *Thou*. My point is that they say nothing about forcing your sinning neighbour to obey them. The only reason to do that is to gain kudos in God's eyes. Sucking up to teacher was always considered creepy in my day."

He puffed, and smoke filled the space between us. "After all, God is also supposed to have said, 'Vengeance is mine.' Surely, even the devout should not presume to take His place."

He swung round, and there was a momentary suggestion of instability, which he circumvented by sitting down heavily. "I took care to explain that to her husband at one Board meeting," he said. "He nearly had his stroke ahead of mine."

He crossed one leg over another, adding, "There are two essential questions. The first is: Should religion listen to the world or the world listen to religion? Which is to be the master?"

"Religions are deaf, so that answers that," Dr. Van said.

"That's the difference between us. I'm an optimist. History tells us that religions change to accommodate."

There was a silence, which Dr. Van broke with, "And what's your second question, Lee?"

Leander shook himself. "Hippocrates was wrong. Do you know why?"

"No." I was intrigued.

"He said, 'Do good or do no harm,' when he should have said, 'Do good or do as little harm as possible.' That's why abortion is only a relative sin. We're doing as little harm as we can in the circumstances. No one ever benefited by being an unwanted child or an unwilling mother. I told Cooper's wife that, too."

I was starting to get some sense of what a hard man Leander would be to cross.

We talked about the hospital, and he recounted battles he had fought with the administration, with Dr. Cooper, with Sister Corrigan. Eventually he put his hand on my shoulder and said, "Those protests a few years back must have been a life-changing experience."

"Yes," I said, "but not as life-changing as working in Sweport."

"That sounds like the truth. Why?"

I told him about the boy with meningitis, the one-armed man with tuberculosis — and the difference I'd found between the living conditions of the owners and the seamen who worked for them. "The people here are little better than indentured slaves," I said. "It shook me. The homes they live in are a disgrace. No toilets, no proper heating, and no privacy. It's not necessary and not right."

"But they have God," said Leander.

"No," I said. "They have their Church. That's not the same."

"Don't you believe there's a god?" Dr. Van asked.

"I don't know why I have to decide something like that," I said.

"You sound like Pierre-Simon Laplace," he said. I looked blank. Leander snorted. "Go on, tell us."

Dr. Van grinned and said, "Laplace was explaining celestial mechanics to Napoleon. He had a good handle on how to derive the position and movements of the planets at any given time — a bold step forward. Napoleon's only comment was, 'You have not mentioned God!' Whereupon Laplace replied, 'I had no need of that hypothesis, Sire.'"

Leander went to a bow-fronted sideboard and took out a crystal decanter. "Good for him. That must have taken courage in that day and age." He turned, smiling, and said, "I'm for a whisky against doctor's orders, how about you?"

We talked as we drank. Afterward, I realized that Leander and I had learned a great deal about each other. And that I had enjoyed myself.

As we left I heard Leander say, "You were right," to Dr. Van.

We drove in silence. Dr. Van stopped the car outside Woodie's house. It was evening. It had rained while we were at Leander's. The seawall at the end of the street was shrouded in mist.

As I got out Dr. Van said, "Brian, give me a moment?" He got out and faced me. As he spoke his accent grew stronger. "I'd like you to think seriously about joining my practice as a partner."

I was really taken aback.

Seeing the look on my face he said, "I know it's a surprise, but you feel as I do about Sweport, and how the people are treated here. You went to Paris and Berlin to fight against this kind of exploitation. You can carry on that fight here, in a practical way. Help the women, and you help the men."

"I don't know what to say."

"Just think about it," he said. "There's no rush to make up your mind. Speak to Helena."

27

WOODIE AND I SAT on a bench in the launderette, our clothes in two adjoining dryers. As they went through the wash cycle we'd eaten fish and chips next door, sitting on plastic chairs facing each other. Now we sat side by side, watching our laundry go round and round. I had coffee, and she had tea, both in plastic cups. We used the same spoon to stir the sugar.

"Did you know he was going to ask me to join his practice?"

"No," said Woodie. "I would have told you." That was the truth. She was too straightforward not to have warned me.

"What do you think?"

"You want to do Obs and Gobs. That's a long way from being a GP in a small place."

"Dr. Van thought it would fit with what I'd started out to do with David and the others in Berlin and Paris."

"That's true, if you believe that giving women choices will help make the world a better place. I do — but we've a long haul in front of us. That timing may not suit you." She sat up straight, pressed her hands into her back and said, "It'd be less exciting than a lot of other lines of work, and you'd have to work bleddy hard to get results. Nothing will be easy, here."

I thought a while before saying, "We'd be working together, you and I."

"Yes." She leaned over and kissed me. "But I won't be the cause of you not doing what you really want."

Her machine stopped. Mine kept going.

"How come yours is ready before mine? How come you always win?"

"I'm cleaner."

"Did you put in less money? That would be cheating."

"You let me know what you decide about Dr. Van's offer," she said. "Whatever it is will be right by me."

She had finished folding her clothes before my machine went silent.

"I don't cheat," she said. She was particular about that.

TWO DAYS LATER I was first-on-call. It was quiet, for once. Visiting hours had just finished, and the place was deserted. I sat with George in his cubbyhole, smoking one of his Gauloises. The back of my throat ached.

"I'm giving them up," I said.

"Me, too." He sat bent forward, elbow on knee, the grey, lined skin of his face sagging. There were several butts in the coronation ashtray that stood on the deep shelf of the switchboard. Queen Elizabeth's face was smudged by cigarette ash.

There was a loud buzz. George said, "SweportMaternityhow-canIhelpyou?"

At the same time I heard a car's horn in the hospital forecourt. It honked, went quiet and then repeated its hoarse call.

As the sound died away a loud bang and the sound of metal grating on metal made me jump.

I ran outside. An old, black Citroën, of the type I had seen in the poorer parts of Paris, was rammed up against the front wing of the Daimler ambulance. Its horn sounded again.

As I ran toward it I thought I heard a moan. Out of the corner of my eye a man with a grey pigtail walked unhurriedly through the hospital gates and out of sight.

George ran past me shouting, "What the hell?"

I remembered that the ambulance was his pride and joy. We reached the car at the same moment, just as the horn sounded again. We peered inside together.

"Oh my God!" George exclaimed and stepped back sharply.

I understood why. Lying across the back seat, with her legs wide apart, was Edna. One foot was pressed against the back of the front seat, which, in turn, was rammed against the steering wheel. When Edna straightened her leg, which she did every thirty seconds or so, the horn sounded.

Edna was straightening her leg at regular intervals because of the pain of labour. I poked my head through the car window to get a clearer view and saw her gaping vagina. I could also see that things were terribly wrong.

First, though her labia were not fully effaced, Edna's cervix was fully dilated, because her anus was flattened open. A small amount of smelly faecal material lay on the seat.

Second, the baby's presenting part was not a head, or a pair of buttocks. Instead, a tiny arm stuck out of its mother's vagina. The sight filled me with horror because that meant that the baby's body lay jammed irrevocably across the opening. It was a classic malpresentation.

Third, the arm and the small shoulder just in view were a deep, dusky red, exactly the same colour as the skinned ducks and chickens I had seen hanging in Chinese butcher shops in the East End of London. I knew that, like the unnatural creatures in those windows, this baby was dead.

Edna was semi-conscious. She moaned every time her uterus contracted in a desperate effort to expel its contents. Her belly rose up in an obscene peak with each contraction. Her face had turned blue. Her tongue protruded. Between contractions she lay quiet, hardly breathing.

"Go fetch help!" I shouted to George. "Get Tripti here, now!"

It was an age before help arrived, and it was not Tripti. It was Mr. Cooper.

He brought two nurses with him. One carried a portable sphyg for blood pressure measurement. By that time I had squirmed inside the car, slid the front seats forward and thrown the brick out of the window. I did not know what to do with Edna.

Cooper took one look and said, "Get an IV going, normal saline. Crossmatch two pints of blood — no, no time! Bring two units of O negative." The nurses disappeared.

"I'll be right back," Cooper said.

I wrapped the sphyg's cuff around Edna's left arm. Her blood pressure was sixty over forty, her pulse thready and irregular. Her cardiovascular system was close to collapse.

George appeared with an oxygen cylinder from the ambulance. We put the green plastic mask over Edna's mouth, and I turned the spigot — I did not think that would make any difference to Edna. I did not think she would live, but you never know. When in doubt you do what your training tells you. That's what it's for.

There was silence. Then Edna screamed. Her belly quivered. It gave a great heave and became even more grossly misshapen. I guessed that her uterus had ruptured. Her breath came in rapid gasps.

Cooper reappeared with a large instrument wrapped in brown paper covering. He must have taken it from the autoclave room. The nurse with him, Our Joanie, trundled an IV pole with two bags hanging from it.

"You put up an IV while I do what has to be done," Cooper said.

"Are we taking her for emergency Caesar?" I asked.

"No time," he said.

"I think her uterus has ruptured. She'll bleed to death if we don't," I said.

"No time," he repeated, unwrapping the brown paper to reveal the instrument that looked like a stainless-steel bolt cutter. It was the Richardson's.

"What are you going to do?" I asked.

"Just put up the IV," he said, as he opened the car door and climbed in next to Edna.

"But —" I started to say.

"Doctor, follow my orders or find someone who will," Cooper snarled.

I turned, broke the butterfly out of its package and attached it to one of the bags. "Hold that," I said to the nurse. "I'll inflate the cuff and try to find a vein." It took several minutes, because her veins had collapsed. Finally, I turned back to look inside the car. Nothing had ever prepared me for what I saw, not in life, not in my training.

Cooper had pushed the mouth of the Richardson's into Edna's vagina above the baby's arm. He put his fingers in alongside the metal.

"Don't touch that arm!" I shouted.

"Correct, Doctor. There would be no point. I am looking for the neck," he said. He probed, nodded as if he had solved a problem, took his hand away and, with one firm movement, closed the jaws of the instrument. There was a crunching sound, muted but unmistakable.

I turned my head away and vomited. He had separated the baby's head from its body.

"Get ahold of yourself, man," he said. "I trust the IV is running?"

"Go to hell!" I shouted, as I opened the lock on the IV fully. A nurse arrived with two bags of O negative. It took precious moments to do the swap from saline to blood. In that time Cooper had pulled the remains of the child out of Edna and laid them on the front seat. It must have taken a fair amount of dexterity — but, then, he was Mr. Cooper, FRCS, FRCOG, surgeon, obstetrician, and gynaecologist.

They lay on the seat, red, anatomically correct, but out-of-place pieces of a person who would never be. I watched helplessly as gouts of blood spurted out of Edna and onto the floor of the car. A few moments later, a last faint breath, a yielding sigh, marked her death. She became still.

When Edna's body was finally placed on a stretcher I turned to the blood-soaked Mr. Cooper and asked, "Why did we not do a Caesar? The O.R. is just over there."

"No time," he said.

"You're a liar," I said.

He leaned forward, his face close to mine. "You know nothing and have learned less. There was not enough time, no matter what you think. Anyway," he said, "I gave this wretched whore a better chance than she deserved."

Standing up he said, "Romans 6:23."

"What?" I shouted, as he walked away.

Our Joanie whispered, "The wages of sin is death."

+ + +

WE WORK WELL TOGETHER: Dr. Van, myself, Barbara, and Woodie. The women find us after hours, when we've finished seeing our regular patients. They come from poverty, from hard work, from families where the men risk their lives for a pittance, so that rich captains and richer owners can look down on them. I can never forget that it is more dangerous to be a deep-sea fisherman than it is to be a firefighter, police officer, or miner.

For their wives and widows, gutting fish is dirty, smelly, unforgiving labour — for which they are paid far less than a living wage. Men and women have to make do. They are told that is their lot in life.

The four of us work because we know that these women need access to contraception and sometimes — rarely — to abortions. We provide help and advice, and, sometimes, a chance at independence.

We talk about Edna and the others, and we try to honour their memory. We may not succeed in freeing the women of Sweport, but, as Dr. Van says, "Your reach should exceed your grasp." We *are* reaching; I want you to know that.

Acknowledgements

To Marlene Goldman ("don't put in anything you don't need and don't move furniture"); to Marina Endicott whose unstinting advice really helped turn a would-be into a published author; and to the knowledgeable staff and editors at Freehand who took a chance and took me in hand.